WHAT READERS ARE SAYING:
As posted on FB.com/LaughingGeorge

"[George's] writings of Karsten Field invite me to enter a dimension that seems so real, touches me so deeply, and leaves such an imprint on my heart it is often almost painful to leave...I have come to feel deeply about the characters; allowing them and the storyline to carry me from the things undesirable in this world."

"His writing digs deep into my heart and brings me to a place where I would gladly live all the time...I found this special series of yours- I believe God brought me to them - I have wondered in my own mind what it would be like to be in Allan's position of leaving it all behind and living a plain and simple life. For me this would be an ideal life- not necessarily an easy one but with God involved a good life."

Also by George Michael Loughmueller

SET FREE
THE KARSTEN FIELD TRILOGY BOOK 1

Available in paperback or eBook.

Please visit the publisher on Facebook

FB.com/MillerWords

The Karsten Field Trilogy Book 2

Bound Together

George Michael Loughmueller

MillerWords, LLC
PO Box 1622
Mount Dora, FL 32756

Copyright © 2013, 2016 by George Michael Loughmueller

Second Edition

For discounts on bulk purchases, please contact
MillerWords Educational Sales at
Sales@MillerWords.com

Printed in the United States of America

2 4 6 8 10 9 7 5 3

Library of Congress Control Number: 2016918399

ISBN: 978-0-9982986-2-7

CHAPTER ONE

THE FLOOD

Ben Abrim Zook stood on his front porch. His seventy-something year old joints ached slightly. He lost count of the exact years he had spent on this planet. The number did not matter much to him. They had all been good years filled with God's glory. He witnessed miracles in his time and intended to stay around for a few more, despite the scar on his stomach. The knife of a desperate man left him injured, but not hurt. Ben Abrim's belief in a peaceful way saved that man's life at the risk of his own.

The sun waited below the horizon for Ben Abrim to finish taking stock in Karsten Field. By now, most everyone would be stirring, preparing to start the day. He looked to his right to see candles begin to flicker in a few kitchen windows. They would not burn long, as the sun would flood those big kitchen windows.

To his left, squirrels dashed across the trail that led to his old friend's house, now occupied by

Samuel and Alice Menlach and their twin children. The squirrels disappeared to the north, in the direction of the river.

Down the hill, Ben Abrim could see the roof of the schoolhouse. Beyond that, he pictured in his head the row of shops that served as a connection to the outside world. Ben Abrim quietly gave thanks. He knew Karsten Field was a good Amish community with good Amish homes.

Then he turned his eyes skyward. The last of the stars glistened in the amber. The cloudless sky sent down an unusually cool breeze for a late spring day. Ben Abrim shivered from the gentle touch of air.

He said, "It is time."

In the Howarth home, having a second child did not change the routine too much. Allan woke before Mary most days. He dressed quietly. He used this time for reflection. Some days, it surprised him to scratch an itch on the side of his face and find a beard. In his old life, Allan always kept a close shave. Since his marriage to Mary seven years ago, his beard grew in thick, but more auburn than the gradually thinning hair on his head.

The cool floorboards of the old schoolhouse chilled his feet. Allan looked forward to summer when he could stay barefoot when he was not working. The worn wood beneath him gave him comfort, but he could not say exactly why. He knew the warmer days were still at least a month away, so he did not waste time getting into his work clothes and boots. His routine included heading over to his daughter's for morning chores before work at the school.

His feet would have a chance to warm up while Mary cooked breakfast. Allan would spend that time with Benjamin and Ruth. After Alice and Brett, Allan never expected to have any more children. With Mary, it felt natural to have another. It also felt natural to name the boy Benjamin after his good friend Ben Abrim. Slightly less than two years later, God blessed them again with a little girl. Allan loved being able to raise them in the faith.

After that, Allan did not plan on any more children and Mary agreed. He respected men like Mr. Troyer or the late Tibold Fencil that had newborns at age sixty, or older. Allan did not see that in his future. They had a complete family now and he could not ask for more.

Besides, little Benjamin seemed to have enough energy for three kids. Some days, the lively boy found it to be a challenge staying in his seat for lessons. Allan and Mary worked hard to meet him with the same discipline as his classmates. It did not make it any easier having a niece and nephew almost his same age. Allan loved his grandchildren as much as he loved his children, but when Benjamin was together with the twins, they could invent new ways to be ornery. None of the three misbehaved too badly. They had been blessed with an abundance of curiosity and mischief.

This morning, Benjamin started his mischief early. According to young Ruth, he teased her about her hair.

"Mamm," Ruth shouted from the children's shared bedroom.

Mary had barely risen from bed and had to detour to answer Ruth's call.

"What is it, little one?" asked Mary. Allan listened from down the hall. He thought his wife did a fine job of showing concern through half-closed eyes.

"Mamm," repeated Ruth, this time in a normal speaking voice. She always made it a point to address the person to which she was speaking. Sometimes, it took saying the name two or three times before she could get her thoughts organized. "Mamm, Benny says I have thistle hair. He says I look like a wild bush."

"With snakes crawling out of it," added Benjamin.

Benjamin ran out of the room before his mother could react. He plowed into Allan as he entered the hall. Allan locked onto his son and guided him back into the bedroom. By now, Ruth huddled up to her pillow with her mother sitting on the edge of the bed. Allan knew Ruth cared for snakes about as much as he did and that was very little.

Mary said, "First, do you think you look like a thistle bush?"

Ruth looked to her brother and then back at her mother. She said, "No. I only woke up two seconds ago."

Ruth's exaggerated concept of time amused Allan.

"It doesn't really matter what your brother thinks then does it?" asked Mary. "If we wasted our time worrying about what others thought of us, we would have no time for anything else. It is not important, but you can tell me what is?"

Allan loved the way Mary dealt with the children. He admired her interactions in the classroom, but she had a special touch when it came to their own.

"Obey Gott. Obey Mamm. Obey Datt," said Ruth. She paused between each with a deep nod and did not say the next rule until she completely raised her head.

"And in that order," said Mary. As she got up from Ruth's bed, she gave Allan a teasing nudge.

"We are forgetting one other thing," said Allan. He yanked off Benjamin's straw hat. "Look at this head."

Benjamin tried to cover his own unkempt hair. His freckled cheeks flashed red with embarrassment for being caught.

"While it does not matter how others view you, look how much trouble it caused worrying about someone else, young man. The time you spent teasing your sister, you could have used taking care of yourself," said Allan.

At the breakfast table, Allan finished sharing his thoughts with his children. He enjoyed looking into their deep, imaginative eyes as they tried to grasp his sometimes intangible concepts. He said, "To me, grooming is important, not because of how others see you. Your body is God's body here on earth. You should treat yourself as you would treat God."

"Yes, Datt," said Ruth.

"Yes, sir," said Benjamin through a mouthful of oatmeal.

Allan started to walk to the door after breakfast. Ruth stopped him by wrapping her precious arms around his waist.

"Stay with me," demanded Ruth.

He could almost not resist, but said, "I have to go help your big sister and Samuel do some chores. I will be back before lunch. We will spend some time together then."

"Promise?" asked Ruth.

"Yes, I promise."

Ruth looked outside and added, "It's going rain."

He double-checked his daughter. The sky showed no signs of possible precipitation. Allan said, "It doesn't look like it to me."

In the back of his mind, he did not dismiss the idea. Sometimes his children, especially Ruth, seemed to be in tune with God's plan. Ever since she learned to talk, she would occasionally contribute deeper thoughts than expected for her age. In some instances, she predicted things before they happened, particularly when it came to animals and nature. Her uniquely exhibited behavior did not occur often enough to draw the attention of others, but Allan noticed when it happened.

Allan left through the side door of the schoolhouse. The students always respectfully used the front door, instead of parading through their living area. He looked forward to the brisk walk in the early morning. Allan seemed to almost always run into some forest friends on the way. Deer and fox kept out of sight as the day progressed.

As he headed up the short hill, Allan could hear Mr. Gundy's pigs squealing in the distance off to his right.

Isaac Gundy liked his pigs and his hogs. He liked them in his sty and he liked them on his table. He named each one, but did not grow attached to them like a pet. Mr. Gundy saw an order in God's world. He knew the rain cleansed and the sun warmed. He knew a cow was for milk and beef. But he believed a swine to be special.

The animal gave so much more variety and Mr. Gundy could make each one of these tasty treats. He carved an abundance of ham steaks, pork shoulders, bacon and more bacon. Isaac Gundy liked bacon. His taste for bacon came as close to a prideful act as anything in Karsten Field. He enjoyed two or three slices with every meal.

Unfortunately, the bacon did not like him as much. If Mr. Gundy had ever visited an English doctor, he would have received some disturbing news regarding the state of his arteries. However, he would not be going into the arms of his Maker this day.

Today, Isaac Gundy hefted his large, bacon-fed frame into the perpetual mud of his pigpen. When he brought out the morning feed, his friends normally came running, eliciting happy squeals. This day, they all seemed to want to huddle under the small lean-to intended to cover less than half the number of pigs squeezing under it. Except two made for the open gate. Mr. Gundy managed to pull the gate closed before Ezra and Edna made an escape.

"Where are you going?" he asked. Isaac Gundy knew they would not respond verbally, but that did not keep him from talking to them. He spoke aloud most every day during the morning feeding. He considered it speaking to God and the pigs were his audience. Sometimes, however, he had to speak directly to the pigs, like today.

"Stop this ruching and come eat," he said. He guessed something in this cool spring air caused the unusual behavior. He had seen them act in all manner of ways in his years. He once had a hog with a fancy for eating the other pigs' tails. Spending almost his whole life around swine, he knew they would eat almost anything, but a tail-less pig did not sit right with him. That hog did not end up on anyone's table. Something did not seem right about that to Mr. Gundy.

In the time it took him to fill the trough, two more pigs tried to force their way out of the gate. One of them rooted under the wire that lined the old wooden fence, but it could not dig deep enough. Isaac Gundy pulled his boots through the sludge toward the escapees and they scattered. He had no idea why they acted as they did today. He might guess it was a "weather bug", but he could not see a single cloud, let alone any storm clouds.

Mr. Gundy had other chores to get to, but he stood and watched his animals for a while longer. Eventually, they started to eat. They ploddled over in pairs or three at a time. Whatever scared them must have scared them less than their own hunger.

Before heading to his whetstone and sharpening a few cleavers, Isaac Gundy joined his oldest son in their field for a good day's work.

Allan made it in good time to Alice's house this day. Usually, he would stop to watch a family of raccoons or some other creature. Today, nothing slowed him. He did not see a single animal along his path, not even the squirrels that Ben Abrim watched earlier that morning.

It seemed strange that he did not see anything, but Allan gave it no further thought. Like most days, Allan helped Samuel with the field and livestock, with the intention of being back to the school before lunch. He still had chores to do around the schoolhouse, in addition to teaching. Today, he promised Ruth he would get back to her soon, so he appreciated the faster pace and fewer distractions.

Since Ruth was not old enough to start school yet, Allan tried to make that extra time for her before lunch. After lunch, he took over the lessons so Mary could start dinner. It took a little longer cooking for four than it did for two. Thankfully, he did not have any picky eaters. Allan remembered how fussy Brett used to be. Whenever they went out to eat, Brett's palette consisted of mashed potatoes or macaroni and cheese. Diners at surrounding tables would have thought green vegetables were poison based on Brett's reaction to them. Benjamin and Ruth did not share that same aversion.

With the old Tunstile cabin in sight, Allan looked forward to seeing his grandchildren before Alice escorted them to school. The twins, Isaac and Elizabeth, reminded him so much of Alice and Brett, in the same way that Benjamin and Ruth did. All four of the new, young people in his life often gave Allan pause to think back to his younger days.

He remembered feeling angry a lot as Brett and Alice entered their teenage years. He did not get angry at them, that was a separate issue. He felt angry at losing the innocent children they used to be. He felt cheated that the time passed so suddenly. As the spark of his first marriage faded, he watched his children grow into people he did not recognize. Then, miraculously, God gave it all back to him. Like an "Almighty reset button", he had strong, healthy relationships with all four of his children. Allan intended to live every minute fully and with gratitude. Having Ruth became the proverbial icing on the cake. He knew he could someday look forward to the joy of her wedding in the same way he felt for Alice.

Samuel greeted him from the porch, bringing Allan out of his emotional thoughts.

"Gut morgen! I'll meet you in the barn," he said.

Allan looked to the barn. Still a bit melancholy, he recalled building that barn. He thought it looked brand new, but that could have been his rose-colored imagination. In the house, Allan could hear the cheers of his grandchildren. They must have seen him through the window, he guessed.

He walked in the front door, intercepted by his oldest daughter. Alice looked aggravated. Things did not seem to be going smoothly in this Menlach house this morning. Allan had been to Samuel's parents' house more than once. He witnessed Mrs. Menlach nurture Samuel's siblings with a discipline that Alice had not yet learned.

"The twins do not want to go to school this morning," she said through gritted teeth.

One of the joys of being a grandparent is the pleasure of young children's company without the responsibility of discipline or cleaning. Allan smiled broadly at his daughter, delighted she could experience motherhood at such a young age. If Samuel's parents were any indication, Sam and Alice had quite a few more children to go.

Allan ducked to his knees and proceeded to spoil the twins. He opened his arms wide so Isaac and Elizabeth could jump into them. He thought the love of a child had to be one of God's greatest gifts and probably why he created humans in the first place. Allan did not want to be the bad guy and tell them they had to go to school, but he loved being their teacher also.

"Are you two being helpful to your Mamm this morning?" he asked.

"Yes, Opa," they said in unison. With their small hands running through his beard, he had no reason to doubt their honesty.

He could not keep his balance on his knees, so Allan let the three of them fall back into a seated position. With Isaac on his left thigh and Elizabeth on his right, he looked up at Alice. "Okay, Mamm, do they have to go to school today?"

"Yes," Alice said sternly. She looked to be hiding her laughter.

"Aww," said Isaac.

"Aww nothing," replied Allan. "Your Uncle Ben will be there and I hear he will even have his hair brushed."

"But we want to stay with you and Mamm today," added Elizabeth. Her pleading eyes reminded Allan so much of Alice at that age.

Testing his fortitude, Allan said, "Don't you have work to do? Lessons to study? You know your Mamm will be working hard all day and Opa and Datt will be in the field. Work always comes before play. If you do your work first, you will always be prepared for what comes after."

"What does come after?" asked Elizabeth.

Allan took a moment before answering. It struck him that sometimes children have an insight that most adults lose or take for granted. He knew she meant what comes after work, but it made him think for a moment about God's promise of what comes after this life. That thought caused him to jump back to Ruth's comment about it raining today. Did she have some insight or foresight, he wondered.

The twins cooperated better after playing on the floor with Allan for a few more minutes. Alice took them off to school and Allan headed to the barn. Samuel had already tended to the chickens and gathered two baskets of eggs, one for his home and one for Allan's. Samuel and Alice always shared their bounty and Allan and Mary always said thank you. With the responsibilities of the school, this arrangement worked best for both families. Samuel appreciated Allan's extra hands on the farm and Allan appreciated the freedom to devote more time to the school.

In the field, they worked the ground in anticipation of planting in a few weeks. Every year, they removed several buckets of rocks, yet every year they found more. Allan could not understand where they came from, but when they turned the earth, there they were. He guessed some of them had to come from the winter meteor showers that they watched bundled in blankets with the kids, who were happy to be up past their bedtime.

Sweat started to form on Allan's brow as the sun climbed up into the sky. An unexpected shadow provided some relief. Allan looked up to see a thick, gray cloud passing in front of the sun. This surprised him because of Ruth's comment that morning. No other clouds accompanied this big one and it moved on long before they finished in the field.

Allan left Samuel shortly before lunch. He stayed a little longer than he intended, but an issue with the plow delayed him. Allan thought about his promise to Ruth. However, he had a responsibility to fix the plow with Samuel. As he told Isaac and Elizabeth earlier, work comes before play.

On the walk home, Allan spied a few smaller clouds, but nothing that would indicate rain coming that day. He noticed the broad leaves of many of the trees turned up, exposing their light green side. Ben Abrim told him once that was a sign of coming rain. Ben Abrim seemed to be full of folk lore and sayings. Allan liked them, but he did not think every one of them had to be true.

To Allan's surprise, before he made it back to the schoolhouse, it started sprinkling. A scattering of clouds slowly knitted together, until a low, gray blanket covered the sky. Ruth waited for him outside. She looked up at the clouds with her mouth open and tongue sticking out as far as she could.

"Careful, a bird might fly over," called Allan as he came down the hill.

Ruth turned to him and a smile ignited on her face. She said, "I told you it was going to rain. I was going to save some in a jar for you, if you didn't get back in time."

"Well, I am back in time for lunch," he said. When Allan came close enough, he scooped Ruth up into his arms. "Besides, I would hardly call this rain."

Ruth hugged him. She said, "I don't think the hard stuff will come down for a while yet. Are you going to spend some time with me before lunch? You promised."

"I think we should help Mamm with lunch," said Allan. The classroom also served as a lunchroom for the students. While each child brought their own midday meal, it helped to have the second adult to keep the room clean. Sometimes, the twins needed a little extra help. He could see a dejected look in his daughter's eyes, but he intended to make it up to her later.

Later did not come quite as Allan had planned. The light sprinkling of rain developed into a heavy downpour before class ended for the day. The rain came down with such force that they could not see the closest house at the top of the hill. Allan had to pull double-duty escorting children to their respective homes. He helped one family at a time and the slow, back-and-forth trips took several hours.

Finally, he had only his children and grandchildren left. Samuel arrived, soaked with the brim of his felt hat hanging limp. The material absorbed so much water that the hat barely held its shape. The unrelenting rain provided the only explanation for why the twins were not home yet.

"Isaac, Elizabeth, let us go," said Samuel.

"Take a blanket to cover them," said Mary. "We don't want anybody getting sick and missing school." She winked at the kids and kissed each on the cheek before they excitedly dashed outside.

Watching from the window, Allan saw Samuel have a hard time keeping up with the twins. They could not have been happier and the blanket flapped behind them, defeating its intended purpose. Half way up the hill, Allan could only make out their dark shapes. The curtain of rain only darkened as night came.

Allan did not think the rain could fall any harder, but the next morning he discovered it could. The riotous pounding on the shingles woke him earlier than usual. The windows might as well have been painted over for all the good he could see out of them.

To make sure he was not imagining the storm, he went to the door in his pajamas. The inflow of water drenched him in the time it took to open the door and slam it shut. Allan felt like he had been dunked in the river. Water covered the wooden floor in a widening spray pattern, but thankfully did not splash the rug or couch.

Mary awoke as Allan changed his clothes. She asked, "What about the children? I don't think we should have school in this kind of weather."

He agreed and said as much. "If anybody braves this deluge, I don't think we should turn them away. I am sure they will have sense enough to stay home."

The people of Karsten Field did have the good sense to stay home. They stayed home for the next four days as the rain kept up a frenzied pace. Finally, on Saturday, it let up somewhat. The rain came nowhere near stopping, but it slowed enough that Allan could see Ben Abrim and Amos Menlach making their way down the mud-covered hill.

He let them in and the men stood dripping for a minute.

"No one has accomplished anything since the start of this deluge," said Ben Abrim.

"We are intending to visit my son and your daughter," added Mr. Menlach. "We have talked with others and think if the rain is so bad tomorrow that we each should keep church in our home."

"I'll go out and talk to Alice. Check on the kids," said Allan. "That's too far for you two in this weather."

Ben Abrim started to smile and then let his lips fall into a frown. "What do you think we are? A couple of alters tumbling down the hill. We have seen it rain before."

Allan had not intended to insult his friend and suspected his feelings were not truly hurt. He jokingly said, "Sorry, I must have mistook your graybeards for something else. If you would like to walk those miles in this rain, don't let me interfere."

"We cannot miss the spring planting. It has to stop sometime," said Amos Menlach.

"Not for forty days," said Ruth from behind her breakfast plate.

Ben Abrim turned his customary grin on her. Allan noticed he always seemed to favor her over the other children. Ben Abrim asked, "What would make you say that?"

Ruth pushed herself away from the table and dashed over to Allan. She must have felt more comfortable in his arms when talking to the other men. She explained, "Noah has forty days of night in the rain to sail away with the animals."

"Gott is gut," said Ben Abrim. "You know of Noah and God's promise."

"Aunt Alice read it to me," Ruth confirmed.

Mary said, "It may be time to study it again."

Both Ben Abrim and Amos Menlach looked delighted at Ruth's knowledge. Mr. Menlach said, "I do not think it will rain for forty days."

As he said this, thunder roared like someone opening a floodgate and the rain grew in intensity.

Ben Abrim looked out the window. He scratched his head and turned to Allan. He said, "In second thoughts, I will take you up on your offer to check on your children. That distance may be too far for my old frame." He winked and put a hand on his lower back to fake some pain.

Then he added, "Mr. Howarth, perhaps you should consider bringing your family to stay with me until the worst of this storm passes."

"Thank you, I will consider it. Now get yourselves home before you get washed away," said Allan. He followed the two men to the door and hurriedly closed it behind them as they ducked out into the rain.

Mary looked concerned. She said, "Should we go stay with him?"

"I don't think that will be necessary. He is being overly cautious. Like Mr. Menlach said it can't rain for forty days," said Allan. He took his wife's hands and added, "We're not going to float away."

"Keep in mind, mein herz, we are at the bottom of the hill and water flows downward," said Mary.

His wife always had a gentle way of expressing her opinion. He did not want her to worry. However, he thought checking on Samuel, Alice and the twins should be a priority. He would have to make the journey on foot, regardless of the storm.

Ten days later, the rain had not stopped. Allan could not remember a time in recent years that it had rained so much. The last time it had come down this much had to be in ninety-three, the year before Alice was born. Allan remembered floods across Iowa from the Mississippi River to the Missouri River. Ben Abrim had intimated they may be in for flooding, but Allan did not think that was going to happen. It now rained for fourteen consecutive days and Allan guessed that had to be a record.

They managed to have school a few of those days, but not much else got done. Allan and Samuel tried to work the field, but they only pushed mud around with their boots. The animals still needed feeding and the cows needed milking.

One afternoon, the rain subsided almost to a trickle. Samuel and Alice brought the twins over for lunch.

"They have been climbing the walls," Alice confided to Mary. "They need something to get this energy out of their system."

Mary looked out the window for a moment and Allan could tell what she was thinking. She said, "One day in the rain would not hurt them, I think. What say you, husband?"

All four children froze in place. Allan could feel their eyes lock onto him as he prepared to answer. He said, "Great, let's go play outside."

Without hesitation, Isaac led Elizabeth, Benjamin and Ruth out the door. Mary could not get to them fast enough to have them put on coats or boots. The children splashed barefoot in the mud.

For a short while, they seemed pleased to dance and enjoy the shower. Then Benjamin discovered he could duplicate snowballs with mud. With Mary and Alice inside, Allan had to decide if he would allow the mudslinging. The outrageous laughter made it easy for him. Allan joined in the fun.

Isaac attempted to escape a particularly large glob by running up the hill. The incline proved too slippery and he came down the hill on his backside. When the other kids saw this, they all scrambled up the hill. They each took turns sliding down the mud runs, covering their clothes and faces in the muck.

Allan could not remember when he had so much fun. He raced to the top to take his turn. As he prepared to slide, he saw Mary waiting at the bottom of the hill. She did not look happy. Everyone froze and the continuing raindrops started to rinse their faces.

Mary shouted, "Mr. Howarth, please come here at this moment."

Feeling giddy, he made a choice that, in retrospect, may not have been the best one. He dropped to his backside and whooshed down the hill. A rooster tail of mud and water fanned out behind him. He moved faster than the kids, probably because of his size. Before he could control himself, his feet met his wife's. The collision took her off her feet and they rolled together to a stop. Allan saw mud caking Mary's hair and face.

At first, he thought she was going to cry, but then she started laughing. They shared a joyful moment together. Samuel and Alice watched from the relative dryness of the doorway, both giggling with delight.

The rain started to come harder again, putting an end to their entertainment. Mary oversaw the kids' return to the house. She had them undress outside, leaving the majority of the mud with their clothes. The pouring rain helped with cleaning their little bodies. Alice brought them in one at a time for warm, dry clothes.

Benjamin insisted on being last. When his turn came, Allan teased his wife. He said, "Mrs. Howarth, exactly how are you going to get inside without muddying up the place?"

Before she could answer, Mr. Gundy's oldest son, Eli, came running. He called, "Mr. Howarth, Mr. Menlach, please come. My father needs you."

Two thoughts flashed through Allan's mind. First, he worried that the bacon-loving Isaac Gundy was having a heart attack. Secondly, for some reason, he wondered why Eli called Samuel mister. He took that moment to appreciate the respect that the people of Karsten Field had for each other. Samuel did not have that many years over Eli, yet the younger boy showed respect even in an apparent time of crisis.

Allan and Samuel left their wives and children to help their troubled neighbor. At the top of the hill, an unexpected sight caught Allan's attention. He had not been up here in a few days to see the effects of the rain on the river. It now churned high above its normal banks. The worried look on young Eli's face kept Allan from thinking any more about the river.

At the Gundy house, Allan felt relief that it turned out not to be a medical emergency. He did become somewhat disheartened when he discovered the cause of the distress. Gundy's pigs rushed the gate and now ruched all over the upper part of Karsten Field.

"Please, help your neighbor," asked Mr. Gundy.

Allan could say nothing except, "Of course. We can catch them."

His optimism turned out to be quite deluded. Max and Reimy Troyer, along with John Lenaxel joined Allan, Samuel and Eli Gundy in an attempt to gather the agitated animals. Ben Abrim watched from his covered porch while Mr. Gundy shouted instructions to the Karsten men running this way and that. Younger children and their mothers watched from other porches and windows. The event proved to be quite humorous except for the men in the rain.

Allan discovered chasing the hogs was easier than trying to collect the smaller pigs. The hogs required at least two men to stampede them back to the pen. All the while, Mr. Gundy called them by name, attempting to coax them back.

Eli Gundy dove for a piglet that squirmed out of his grasp. It proceeded to run between Max Troyer's legs before Samuel caught it by the hind legs. The grunts and squeals of the panicking pigs mingled with the growing laughter of the audience. With almost half the swine recovered, the chore felt more like a game to the men and they shared in the amusement.

The rain let up again, which aided in the capture of the slippery escapees. Then some of the mothers allowed the younger boys out to help their brothers and fathers. Inseparable friends

Simon Otto and Malachi Miller rode one of the largest hogs back to the pen, guided by Allan. He watched the boys slide off into the mud, most likely on purpose.

Eventually, they prodded the last hog through the broken gate. Mr. Gundy waited with a hammer and nails to secure the pigs. Mrs. Gundy offered towels and hot tea to the wild-looking, mud-covered men standing under the buggy awning.

Allan looked one house over to see Ben Abrim's always smiling face bobbing in and out of sight. He took to rocking in his chair as the activity came to a close.

Then an incredible roaring caused everyone to fall silent. Somehow, Ben Abrim must have known what was coming. He stood from his rocker and calmly said, "This is it."

The old man looked across the way. Allan followed his gaze and could see the river now almost up to the back of the Fencil house. It swirled with fury. Allan guessed that either a levee broke or someone upriver, probably miles away, opened it. Allan followed the rush of the churn and watched it crest at the top of the hill. The mud slides that he and the children created made natural channels for the overflowing water. Even without the channels, the waves easily crested the hill.

"We have to get back to the schoolhouse," Allan shouted to Samuel over the heads of the other Karsten men. Samuel came without question.

As they came to the muddy road that led down to his home, Allan realized that Eli Gundy and John Lenaxel followed to help. Another surge of water poured down the hill behind them. Almost a foot of water took the Lenaxel boy off his feet, hurtling him down the hill. Samuel got to the boy and pulled his head above water. Allan and Eli Gundy made it to the schoolhouse, wading through the standing water.

Further down the road, Allan spotted Mr. Kinzinger and his family struggling with their wagon. The horse did not appear to want to cross the rising water.

"Come with us," called Allan, hoping they could hear him over the roaring water.

Mr. Kinzinger yelled back, "We are going to the restaurant."

Allan had to let it go at that. He knew the shops were higher than where they were now and hoped they would be safe.

He turned back to his home. Mary stood in the doorway, holding Ruth. Water swallowed the top step, inches from going into the house. He grabbed Ruth. Mary went back inside for Benjamin. Then Alice came to the door with the twins. By then, Samuel and John Lenaxel caught up and took Isaac and Elizabeth. Allan helped his oldest daughter down into the water. His mind raced at the slightest possibility of losing any of his children. Eli Gundy held Mary by the arm as they left the house.

Another torrent capped the hill making it extremely difficult to get back to the top. Allan led the way, almost squeezing the breath out of Ruth. He lunged from tree trunk to tree trunk, praying not to slip. Mary latched onto her husband and Eli Gundy followed her with Benjamin clinging to his back. They formed a human chain and helped each other up the hill.

Close to the top, Allan's knees almost failed him. He had never been more frightened. If he fell now, he would likely drown. Worse than that, he could lose Ruth. Her small body could not withstand the raging current. She would be gone before he could react.

Allan prayed silently in his head. He knew God had given him strength to walk a difficult path. He gave thanks for the beautiful gift of his children and asked to save them for better things. Then, under the frigid water, he felt a warmth rising from his feet. Without warning, he had renewed strength in his legs. He trudged up the rest of the precarious hill without another misstep.

The rest of the short walk became a blur in Allan's memory. He would later think that it stopped raining only on the path in front of them and only long enough for them to get to Ben Abrim's front porch. The Elder of Karsten Field welcomed them with open arms and dry blankets.

Ben Abrim said, "I am glad you took me up on my offer. Next time we will be prepared, yah?"

"I pray there will not be a *next time*," answered Allan.

That night, Ben Abrim seemed to enjoy the company of two additional families in his home.

Exhausted children occupied various pieces of furniture, while the parents made due with blankets on the floor. Before she fell asleep, Ruth snuggled with her father. Allan enjoyed the attention amid snores and deep breathing.

"You finally get to spend some time with me," said Ruth.

The idea that it took a flood for him to make time for his daughter stung. Allan knew his duty and God always came first, but he would not let work come before family again. He would not shirk his responsibilities, but being a father was one of them.

It rained for another three days.

When the rain ended, Ruth spotted a joyous surprise that morning. They left Ben Abrim's house in anticipation of inspecting the damage to their own. Riding on her father's shoulders, Ruth looked up into the sky. She had seen rainbows before, but Allan agreed this one seemed more vibrant and radiant than any even he had seen. The tapestry of colors stretched in a full arch across the southern sky. The dark clouds drifting away behind it only made the rainbow seem that much more intense.

"It's God's promise," said Ruth.

"Yes it is," said Allan. He firmly believed that God had a plan for Karsten Field. He did not think a flood or tornado could wipe them off this land.

All of the pigs survived, but Mrs. Otto lost a few chickens. The Kinzingers made it safely to the restaurant and offered to share their store of canned foods. Samuel and Alice found their house completely dry. The flood did not come close. The overflow from the river washed away a chunk of the hill before it dropped back into its bed. This dip inspired Mr. Esch, the furniture maker, to want to build a bridge over it.

Surprisingly, the schoolhouse took very little damage. Water did make it inside, but judging from the baseboard, Allan surmised that there was no more than an inch of standing water in the classroom. The old house would need some kind attention, but he figured they had plenty more years left in it.

Most everything, except the pigpen, dried. That year's planting started late, but Karsten Field still had a fine harvest. Many years later, after Ruth had children of her own, she would see Ben Abrim's empty house and fondly remember why it reminded her of Noah and his ark.

CHAPTER TWO

ATTAINABLE

Sometimes, in the early morning hours before the sun started to warm the tops of the trees, Allan would tip toe down the hall. His daughter, Ruth, would wake before him on a rare occasion. He liked to push open his children's bedroom door only a crack and watch them.

This morning, despite the relentless heat of the past weeks, the wooden floor sent goose bumps up Allan's back and down his arms thanks to his bare feet. He made his quiet trek with the hopes of catching a glimpse of Ruth's special world. He longed to see through her eyes and experience the wonder of this world that God put before her as something new. Her outlook revived him on a daily basis.

Benjamin left the door ajar after his trip for that *one last* drink of water that every child needs before sleep. That made it easy for Allan to peek into the room without being noticed. He could hear a whisper. It sounded like a mother speaking to her child.

Allan pressed his face deeper into the darkness.

The smell of the wooden door momentarily distracted him. The old wood made him wonder who might have cut and hung the solid oak, probably before he was born. His daughter said something. He could not hear exactly what, but it drew his attention. The moon had already set and the sun had yet to join them. That left the room indecipherable. Somewhere in the black, he knew Ruth played with her doll.

Mary sewed it for Ruth's third birthday. His wife had a fine hand when it came to a stitch, but this was her first attempt at making a doll. In her years of teaching, Mary had not made a single doll for any of her students. Her skill lay in mending. Regardless of the lack of experience, the result made Ruth excitedly happy. The little girl took cues from her mother and raised her doll in a mirrored fashion. If Mary hugged, or disciplined, Ruth, then the doll received the same treatment from its *mother*.

Allan watched in amazement how deeply his wife cared for their children. It pleased him that his youngest daughter already shared that love with others. Benjamin did not disappoint in that area either, but he was a boy and preferred to act as boys will.

Allan leaned a little farther into the room. He wanted to hear what story or lesson Ruth shared with her doll this morning. He held firmly to the doorframe to keep from stumbling into the room. He could feel the wood, worn smooth from years of children's hands rubbing over it as they dashed or swung or slipped through the doorway. The wearing away seemed to move up as his children aged. At some point, he knew it would stop. For now, he did not mind it so much.

Leaning into the room, he could hear Ruth a little better. Either she did not know he was there, or she did not mind.

"How do you get such tangles?" Ruth asked. No response came from the patchwork doll, but she acted as if it did. "If you would hold still for a moment, I could be done by now."

Allan found his peace years ago. He took pleasure in knowing God's grace. While he still walked this earth, he would know joy through his children. Ruth's simple playtime gave him extra energy for an already blessed day.

Then, he thought he heard a different voice. Ruth said something about her baby needing a new dress, but it did not sound like Ruth. He thought he heard Alice in that room. Not Alice now. Not the mother of his grandchildren. The voice seemed to come from a million miles away and a million years ago. When Alice was a little girl, she had the same problems with her dolls. They often needed new dresses, not because she wore them out, but because she mangled them. As a five-year-old, Alice already had an eye for fashion. So many Barbie outfits came to a cruel end at her blunt nose scissors.

With Alice and Brett, and now Benjamin and Ruth, he would sometimes catch a glimpse of the adult they would become. A facial expression or movement would reveal their future selves. Allan always looked for those bittersweet moments. Rarely did it work backwards. For an instant, Ruth's voice took him back to his younger self, a new, clueless father. He realized back then that he did not know what to do with a daughter. In some ways, he felt the same now.

God had blessed him with boys and girls. As for Brett and Benjamin, Allan thought he knew how to handle them. He could do the things that boys do, the things that he did as a boy.

Girls.

Girls confused him. He worried for months at how fragile Alice seemed. That long unused, but not forgotten, anxiety returned with Ruth. After two daughters and a second marriage, women still remained a mystery that Allan made no progress at solving. He decided his only hope would be to love them unconditionally and serve them as best he could. The rest, he left up to God.

"Yes, I love you too," said Ruth speaking to her doll. Then she sucked in a breath, an action of false surprise. "Datt, she has a loose tooth."

Ruth calling out to him startled Allan. He wondered how long she knew he was there. He came into the room and sat in the pale pink rectangle cast from the hint of sun starting outside the window. The doll had no mouth, but Allan stuck out his calloused index finger all the same. He waited for Ruth to guide it, her small hand wrapping completely around his finger. In his heart, she wrapped him around her little finger.

When he touched the doll and pretended to feel the wiggling tooth, Allan went into convulsions. He shook his entire body in a gesture that meant he could not stand the feel of a loose tooth. He did this with Ruth for the first of her teeth to calm her fears. She giggled uncontrollably then and it still worked now.

The laughter stirred Benjamin from sleep. The boy had lost his share of teeth, including one before its time. Even with four children, Allan successfully managed to avoid pulling a single tooth. The sudden movement of something that normally does not move somehow unnerved him. The sensation sent a spark down his spine much to the delight of his children.

Allan left the room carrying a boy, a girl and a baby doll. They would breakfast together before Allan went out into the heat of another summer day, a summer that desperately lacked rain.

It had recently been too hot to do anything. The horses seemed reluctant to shoulder their harnesses. The cows acted as if they did not want to be touched. The men did not complain. They did not honestly want to be out in the unbearable heat either. Still, work had to be done, so much prayer was devoted to a consensus for rain. They gave much thanks for the excess of rain brought that previous spring and asked that some of it could be shared now. The flood caused a delay in their planting and now this drought could ruin their crops entirely.

The Karsten men did their best with what they had. Allan conceded that the weather was beyond his control. He knew he walked with the Lord in Karsten Field. He knew what God touched could not fail. All the same, he gave thanks that today was Saturday.

Allan worried that he could not spend another day toiling in temperatures over one hundred and five degrees. The thermometer hanging by the classroom door confirmed ninety degrees by eight in the morning every day that week. The swirling dust in the fields dried his nose and throat. Most of their planting withered before it was knee-high. Yet every Karsten man that had a responsibility to be outdoors made it outdoors each day. It impressed Allan and encouraged his heart to see it. These men had to take care of their families and did it with whatever God provided.

Fishing at the river had been a tradition on Saturdays for some time. With the current drought, the men did not go for leisure so much as necessity. Allan carried two spare buckets to bring back extra water from the distressingly low river. Previous summers, the men could cast their lines from the shade of the nearby trees. These past several weeks, Allan had to walk out onto the exposed riverbank simply to get his feet wet. Not that the brittle leaves provided much shade.

Allan would have preferred leaving before sunrise. Today, however, Ruth asked if she could join her father. Normally, Allan could say yes without concern.

"What does Mamm think?" asked Allan. He tried to convey concern in his expression to his wife.

Mary stopped her work at the counter. It looked to Allan like she had the beginnings of a pie. He did not envy her having the oven on for any reason. However, she intended to bring food to the Otto's house for church tomorrow. If Allan knew anything, he knew that Mary's mind could not be changed once it had been set on something.

Mary wiped her hands on her apron and leaned over to Ruth. She said, "Mamm thinks you could go for a bit and dunk your barefeets in the water. Don't let your Datt fall asleep in the grass."

"I don't see that happening," said Allan. He tried to envision himself on the crunchy, yellow grass with his hat pulled over his eyes. He would have a better chance of resting comfortably with Mr. Gundy's pigs. At least there, he would be cooler in the mud, even with the knowledge of how the pigpen stayed wet. He asked his wife, "Do you think it will be too hot for the small ones?"

"These days, it is hot inside and out. Take your children and come home before lunch. That will not be too much sun for them," said Mary.

Benjamin, who had previously seemed uninterested in the conversation, said, "I can carry your pole."

"I can carry the water bucket," added Ruth.

With that, the decision had been made. The father left the house with one child carrying a bucket and the other, his fishing pole. His kids did not seem to mind walking on the warm ground without their shoes. However, Allan did not want to be shoeless, standing on slippery rocks, wrangling with a fish, if he caught one. They intended to fill their buckets, one with water, and the other, hopefully, with fish.

Allan also intended to fully enjoy the extra time with his children. In the back of his mind, he worried somewhat about the heat. Slightly before nine, the thermometer offered them close to eighty-eight degrees and climbing. By the time they made it to the top of the hill, Allan could already feel the sweat forming under his hatband and dripping down the back of his neck.

Ben Abrim waved at them from the Fencil's front porch. It looked like he and Matthew, the late Elder Tibold's oldest, were having a conversation. From the anguished look on Ben Abrim's face, Allan could guess about what. The topic of the drought occupied many discussions in Karsten Field.

Allan detoured his kids toward Ben Abrim and Matthew. He did not want Ruth or Benjamin worrying about their situation, so he hoped to talk briefly and vaguely with the other two men.

"It is insurmountable. We have no chance," said Ben Abrim. For once, Ben Abrim did not have a smile on his face. His words took the smiles off Benjamin's and Ruth's faces too. Allan wanted to avoid the details because he knew they would be exaggerated in their young minds.

"You've been out in the sun too long," Allan tried to joke. He knew their situation was not a joke. He never knew Ben Abrim to waver in such a way. Allan knew the drought had slowly been killing their crops, but he saw no sign to panic. It looked like his friend was on the verge of panic.

"I pray, Mr. Howarth. You know I do," said Ben Abrim. "If this is God's will, then so be it. With all that we've lost this year, I know for certain we do not have enough food for winter. Nor do we have the seed for spring planting."

Ruth tugged on Allan's pant leg. She asked, "What does he mean, Datt?"

Allan put his hand on Ruth's head. This technique worked well with her and Benjamin to let them know when they were interrupting. As long as he kept his hand there, Ruth knew to wait patiently.

"Have you spoken with everyone?" Allan asked Ben Abrim. The older man nodded. Then Allan turned his attention to his daughter. He said, "It only means that we will all have to work a little harder. Why don't you and your brother take our things down by the river? I will follow you in a moment."

Ruth seemed satisfied with Allan's answer. Benjamin took the second bucket from his father and the siblings hurried away. Their laughter at the anticipation of splashing each other held more weight for Allan than Ben Abrim's troubling news.

He turned back to his friend and said, "Mr. Zook, I have never seen you like this."

Ben Abrim patted his cheeks with an already damp handkerchief. Allan knew his friends sweated as much from anxiety as heat.

"I am shaken, Allen," he said. "I realize my words are out of turn. I must surely sound blasphemous. For all of the summers I have seen, I have not seen one hurt us so close."

"There have been droughts before," said Allan. He placed a hand on Ben Abrim's shoulder and could feel him trembling.

"True, but even as a child, thank God, He provided. I cannot recall something so bad," said Ben Abrim.

Allan did not like to see his friend in a state of doubt. He knew first hand of the dying crops. The unrelenting heat withered so many stalks in his son-in-law's field. It had to be the same through all of Karsten Field. Allan heard they had lost a few chickens too, but he did not think things were so dire. They had to have stores of canned goods and Mr. Kinzinger ordered some supplies for his restaurant.

He said, "Surely God watches over Karsten Field. No one is going to starve. In the worst case, we can ask Mr. Kinzinger to place an extra order on his next delivery."

The suggestion sparked something in Ben Abrim. Allan could see him registering the idea behind his eyes. Then his grim expression returned. Ben Abrim said, "We will talk with Mr. Kinzinger. First, let me tell you something of faith. Because we believe, then we are on the path to Heaven. Our independence from technology frees us from the burden of temptation and sloth. However, that same technology will save other farms this summer. We did not bring God to this land. He was already here and He decides what to do with it. Because we have faith, does not mean He will solve all of our problems. In our life, we will know pain, hunger, sorrow. God may not keep us from suffering, but He will not let us go through it alone. Our reward is not a perfect life now; it is a perfect life once we are called to Him. Do you see now why I am concerned?"

It did make sense to Allan. Ben Abrim cared more for every member of Karsten Field than himself. His heart must be aching at the thought of any of the children going hungry.

Ben Abrim continued, "Show others that the Lord is here. We must do the work in our time and He will provide the proof in His. Go; spend time with your children. After lunch, come with me to Mr. Kinzinger's and we will discuss your idea."

Allan carried Ben Abrim's words with him to the river. Each time he felt like he had things figured out, God taught him a new lesson. Allan chided himself for thinking God would provide what they needed only because they believed. Did he allow himself to think that God was obligated to save them in this existence? Does God not so love all the world that he gave his only son?

At the river, he found Ruth and Benjamin playing on the riverbank. Both had mud up to their knees and flush red cheeks. A combination of running and heat slowed them to their current resting spot. Allan sat beside them. "Pray with me, children," Allan said.

"Yes, Datt," said Ruth.

Both kids climbed onto their father's lap and closed their eyes. Ruth squeezed her eyes shut, but Benjamin peeked as he often did. He seemed to like watching his father when they prayed together. Allan did not speak aloud, but in his heart, he asked that his arrogance be forgiven.

After a silent moment, Ruth pried open Allan's eyes with her gentle fingertips. He held back a few tears. He taught his children that it was okay to cry, but he did not want to frighten them.

"Look what I found," said Ruth.

Focusing on her small hand a little too close to his face, Allan saw five stones. Each round rock looked smooth and very different from others that Allan found near the river. Each one looked yellow and had been worn round as if the river did it purposefully. Carefully balanced and hanging past the end of her fingers, she held all five in one hand.

"What are those for, mein herz?" asked Allan.

Ruth carefully and deliberately pointed her finger, touching each stone as she explained. She said, "This one is for Mamm and Datt. This one is Benjamin and me. Here is Alice, Samuel, Isaac and Elizabeth. This one is for Ben Abrim. And this is everyone else in Karsten Field."

"Aren't you forgetting someone?" asked Allan.

She pondered for a moment, quietly counting the stones. Finally, she asked, "Who?"

"Which one is God?"

"God's not a little rock, silly. He's the river," said Ruth.

He's the river. The idea seemed so simple to Allan. Of course God is the river. He shaped the stones and carried them on their journey. It amazed Allan that his young daughter could think of something so complex, yet so obvious.

Then another thought clicked in Allan's head. King David once held five stones. He only needed one when he faced a giant that invaded God's lands. David did not need all five rocks, but he had to be prepared. He believed God would guide his hand and stop Goliath with one stone. However, that was David's plan and David did not know God's plan. Having the extra stones did not limit God to only one outcome. David had to trust that God knew the best outcome. Right now, the people of Karsten Field faced their own Goliath. Allan did not know if the drought would destroy Karsten Field. Maybe they could find some way to win, or maybe they would not. Looking at those small stones in his daughter's hand gave Allan renewed strength.

He trusted God.

After a light lunch, Allan wanted to talk to Mary about the situation. She continued to make extra food for church and Allan thought there would be no harm in holding back some.

"We still have to eat tomorrow," said Mary. She seemed adamant about her plans.

Allan tried to keep his voice low since the kids were playing in the next room. They were supposed to be getting ready for a nap, but that looked unlikely to happen. He said, "We need to eat this winter too."

"If that is his plan, then we shall eat then too," said Mary. She obviously did not share the same concern as Ben Abrim.

Originally, Allan did not think there was cause for alarm. Talking to Ben Abrim drew attention to it. He pulled his wife close and wrapped his arms around her. She let her head fall to his chest. Her attitude and support helped calm his nerves. He had decided at the river to leave it up to God and her reassurance strengthened his resolve.

"As David prepared for all possible outcomes, I will go with Ben Abrim to Kinzinger's restaurant. It may be His plan to send us outside help," explained Allan.

Before Allan left the house, he checked on the kids. Benjamin had actually fallen asleep. His feet hung halfway off the bed. The heat made them all tired and it looked like the boy surrendered in the middle of his playtime.

Ruth, however, sat on her bed, wide-awake. She watched a bee flutter in and out of her open window.

"It can't find any flowers," she said.

Allan smiled and said, "You better be careful then. You are sweeter than a flower. Your friend may come after you."

Apparently, Ruth did not like his teasing. She sprang from her bed and hid behind her father. She peeked around him once to make sure the bee went back out the window.

"Back to bed with you," said Allan. "I am off to Mr. Kinzinger's."

"May I please go with you, Datt?" begged Ruth.

She did not look sleepy at all. Allan figured the walk would tire her and get her to bed all the earlier tonight. He worried a little about getting her there in the heat. Then he remembered the restaurant had air conditioning. Mr. Kinzinger kept the central air, like the telephone, for the convenience of his guests. If this indulgence saved his daughter from possible heat stroke, then he would both repent and give thanks later.

In the restaurant, the sudden change in temperature gave Ruth goose pimples. Mr. Kinzinger never set the thermostat below seventy-eight. Compared to outside, it felt like winter to Allan. He once doubted he could get used to living without air conditioning. He used to sleep with his own thermostat set below seventy. For Allan, sixty-three would be an ideal temperature for an August night, but his first wife, Tina, would never allow it. Now the artificially cool air felt foreign to him. He overcame that like so many other weaknesses in his life.

Allan joined Ben Abrim and Martin Kinzinger at one of the several vacant tables. They rarely saw other diners at this time of day. Ruth had her choice of tables. Once she chose one by the window, Mrs. Kinzinger brought her a glass of lemonade. Ruth had her doll to keep her company, so Allan could concentrate on the conversation already in progress.

With the exception of Allan, Martin Kinzinger probably had the most experience in dealings with the English. He opened his restaurant in the early seventies. As farming technology changed, the people of Karsten Field had to find new ways to keep their farms going. Mr. Kinzinger did not run the restaurant for a profit. Any money he made went to purchase livestock, replacement parts for their plows and cultivators, and of course, his utility costs.

Martin Kinzinger served as the unofficial Treasurer of Karsten Field. He negotiated the contracts for Gundy's pigs and Mr. Esch's furniture. If Karsten had a chamber of commerce for their row of businesses, Mr. Kinzinger would be the president. He consolidated all of the electric bills from each shop. He even found a company to put up a windmill. He constantly had to remind others that the Englishers called it a *turbine*. This *turbine* fed electricity back into the meter, making their stores a little less dependent on outside help.

"When I say there is no money, then there is no money," finished Mr. Kinzinger.

Ben Abrim looked dismayed. "There has to be some," he said.

Kinzinger pushed a plate of half-eaten pie to the side and folded his hands on the table. He leaned forward and spoke softly. "Business has been slow. Mr. Esch has received less than half of his usual Christmastime orders. We still have a few months for that to increase, but the English are having what they call a *recession*. Mr. Troyer's Bed and Breakfast has not had one guest this summer."

Allan stayed busy with the school and his family. They did not often have a reason to come down to the shops. He did not realize business had been so bad. He suspected he had a better understanding of their situation than Ben Abrim grasped.

"Can we not order more food from your restaurant supplier?" asked Ben Abrim.

"There are no funds to do that. As things are, Mrs. Kinzinger and I are going to close for winter at the first of October. We cannot afford to order the supplies," said Mr. Kinzinger. He shifted in his seat. "Think on this. If there is no harvest, then there is no grain. What shall we plant come spring? You know as well as I, Mr. Zook, that Karsten Field has never faced a trial such as this."

Before Ben Abrim could express his concern, the front door bell chimed. The three men turned toward the front of the restaurant. Ruth stopped playing with her doll. The pleasant ringing even brought Mrs. Kinzinger out of the kitchen.

A dark skinned man, woman and boy stood in the doorway. They looked as wide-eyed and uncomfortable as they could possibly be without screaming and running out the door. Allan guessed they did not expect a greeting of total silence.

He corrected that immediately with "Welcome friends. Come in. This is Mr. Kinzinger's restaurant.

Allan gestured to Kinzinger and he stood. Apparently, they all shared the surprise of visitors that were so different from them. Mr. Kinzinger said, "I am sorry that lunch is over, but Mrs. Kinzinger can make you something.

The visitors smiled politely and the father urged them toward a table. Allan noticed Ruth staring and it occurred to him that she had never seen African Americans in her young life. Ruth scooted off her bench and made her way over to Allan.

She pulled her father down close for a whisper. "Datt, why is their skin so dark?"

Allan did not know how to respond. He could not think of a way to explain it without possibly offending the guests. Then Ben Abrim seemed to suddenly recover. He flashed his comforting smile that had been absent over the past several days. From his seat, he pulled Ruth to him, first with a hug and then he lifted her onto his lap.

Ben Abrim said, "My dear, the good Lord paints his children in all the colors of the rainbow."

Allan watched Ruth. He tried to get inside her head as she smiled. He knew she would be imagining God literally painting babies. Then the visiting mother smiled too. Apparently, she liked Ben Abrim's expression.

The woman said, "She is a beautiful little girl."

"I thank God and her mother for that," said Allan.

Mr. Kinzinger finally returned to the table and presented the strangers with a pair of handwritten menus held in flimsy plastic sleeves. Mrs. Kinzinger took care to clean the menu holders every day and as a result, they lasted much longer than their supplier would have liked.

"Thank you, but we actually didn't come here to eat," said the man. "My name is William. This is my wife Natasha and our son Chris. Our family name is Bowman. I've come looking for some answers."

Mr. Kinzinger said, "We had some Bowman's some time back. Do you kenn it, Mr. Zook?"

Ben Abrim looked like he did know it. He adjusted Ruth on his lap and a familiar expression dawned on his face. Allan knew his friend had a story to tell.

"It's true. We did have a line of Bowman's that ended here in Karsten Field. The last Mr. Bowman left us some time ago. The English doctors said it was stomach cancer that took him home. If I recall, the family came from back east sometime shortly before my birth." Ben Abrim paused.

Will Bowman looked as excited now as he had looked startled moments ago. "Would that have been in the early forties?" he asked.

"Oh, I don't know for certain, but that should be close," said Ben Abrim.

The visitor stood up and started shaking each of their hands. His excitement grew considerably.

He turned to his wife, "Tash, I think we found them."

In the jostling, Allan looked to Ben Abrim. Ben Abrim winked at Allan. Clearly, the elder knew more about the present situation. After a moment, Will Bowman settled. Allan and Mr. Kinzinger sat down at the next table.

"I've been searching for my family," started Will.

"And now you've found them," finished Ben Abrim.

Clearly, Ben Abrim understood what Will Bowman wanted. Allan now had a need to understand too. He said, "Mr. Zook, if you would kindly explain please."

Ben Abrim indirectly answered Allan by speaking to Ruth. He said, "Young miss, you asked why our new friends appear different from us. That is an old story, not too different from the story of David and Goliath. Do you know that story?"

As Ruth vigorously nodded her affirmation, Allan had to take a breath. King David walked through his thoughts all day. He wondered how Ben Abrim could make that connection with these visitors.

"We plain people stay out of the affairs of the English as much as we can. They have a long history of trouble, strife and mistreating their brothers," said Ben Abrim. "Many years ago, Englishers took people that looked like Mr. Bowman from their homelands and forced them to work. Do you know what a slave is, Ruth?"

Allan's daughter shook her head to indicate she did not know. Allan wondered if it was something he should have taught his children. They did not spend much time teaching history in school, with the exception of the Bible. He and Mary focused on the lessons of Jesus with their students. Although the Bible had many examples of slavery, they never seemed to teach it. Maybe, he thought, he should include it in future lessons.

Ben Abrim continued, "To say it simply, slavery was like Goliath."

"He was a giant?" asked Ruth. She seemed genuinely interested to Allan. He looked at the Bowmans and, apparently, Ben Abrim caught their attention as well.

"No, not a *he*. But yes, it was a gigantic destructive force. Slavery is a terrible thing of both thought and action where one man forces another against his will. I should let your parents explain it to you better," said Ben Abrim. "Brother Joseph Bowman stood up to this giant in his own way. He did not fight in the American Civil War. That is not our way."

Mr. Kinzinger left the table for a moment. He returned with a second serving of pie for himself and enough for everyone else. Ben Abrim continued his story.

Joseph Bowman lived in the free state of Pennsylvania to the west of the Susquehanna River. His wife looked after his six sons and the sons helped work the farm.

Living close to the border of Maryland, seeing slaves was not infrequent. The Bowmans witnessed many unspeakable acts, yet they could do nothing more than pray. Some late nights, at the screams of some lost soul, the family would rise from sleep and pray that the slave would soon find peace in this life or the next. A war was coming and with it came more tortured sounds in the night.

One summer day, Joseph herded his cows into the barn for morning milking. His two oldest boys waited, stools in hand, inside the barn. The four younger boys ran about the field, presumably helping steer the cattle, but more likely enjoying the day.

Mr. Bowman spotted him first. A dark-skinned man in ragged clothes stood at the edge of the southern tree line. He looked weak and frightened. He remained frozen, like a startled deer, when Mr. Bowman waved. Joseph knew this man had to be a slave. They did not see any other dark-skinned people so close to the slave state of Maryland. He guessed that the man must have escaped.

In that instant, Joseph Bowman decided for once that he could help without raising a hand to violence. Being true to his faith, Mr. Bowman declined an invitation to join the Union Army. Naturally, he did not allow his sons to go either.

The English even tried to coax his fifteen-year-old boy into taking up arms. Mr. Bowman found what they had been praying for, a chance to give peace, albeit to only one man.

Joseph sent his youngest to have Mrs. Bowman prepare a bath. The runaway did not move from the cover of bushes. Surely, Mr. Bowman thought, the man did not think he was well hidden, but still he did not move.

Mr. Bowman crossed the field and stopped within ten feet of the scared and scarred man.

"Come, friend. I have food and clean clothes," offered Joseph.

The man did not move.

"You can't stay in the bushes. Surely, someone is looking for you," added Joseph.

The words must have made some sense to the man. He stepped clear of the underbrush and Mr. Bowman saw his scraped and bloody feet. Joseph put an arm around him and the man flinched. The apparent tenderness of the man's shoulders told Mr. Bowman that someone had mistreated this man badly.

In the house, the man soaked in Mrs. Bowman's bath water and voraciously ate half a loaf of bread. He did not speak much, despite the boys' barrage of questions. At least, Mr. Bowman did learn the man's name.

"They call me Marcus," said the escaped slave.

Mr. Bowman made a decision then that would affect Marcus and his family for the rest of their lives.

"Brother Marcus, I can offer for you to stay with us for as long as you need. I will not ask you to share our workload; you have earned some rest. Someday, this hateful institution may pass. Until then, live as part of our family. If anyone comes looking, we will hide you up."

Marcus said thank you that day, more than Joseph heard anyone say it in a given month. His rest did not last long. After a few days of healing, Marcus insisted on helping with chores. He had particularly good experience dealing with the livestock.

Several days later, a group of Confederate soldiers passed by the farm. They asked if the Bowman's had seen any runaways. Mr. Bowman spoke for the family stating they had not. He did not believe any of these men were Marcus's former owners. However, they did insist on searching the house and barn, but found nothing. The Bowman boys made a game out of burying Marcus with straw in the barn loft. The soldiers did not have enough interest in their assignment to take more than a cursory glance. The armed men moved on, presumably to the next farm.

And a few days after that, Mr. Bowman's neighbor told him of the fighting that had broken out in a town called Gettysburg. Joseph and Marcus decided together that it would no longer be safe for him to stay.

"I will go north an' try to find my wife. She 'scaped the day afore I did and I don't know if she is alive, but she ne'r did come back," said Marcus.

"May the Lord be a light unto your feet in these dark times, my friend," said Mr. Bowman.

"That is the story as I kenn it," finished Ben Abrim.

Young Chris Bowman clinked his fork on his empty pie plate.

"Gut, hah," said Mr. Kinzinger. "You like the pie. Mrs. Kinzinger will give you another to take home."

Allan liked the pie too, but he wanted to know how Ben Abrim's story connected to their visitors. "Mr. Zook, do you know what happened after that?"

"I can tell you," said Will Bowman. He looked relieved and ecstatic. Apparently, he had found what he was looking for in Karsten Field, as Allan did. Now he wanted to share it. He said, "The Bowman family moved west after the end of the war. Two generations later, the last members of the family line settled in Karsten Field. I had hoped to meet some of them. I have spent a lot of time and research and can find no other direct descendants of Joseph Bowman."

"Isn't your name Bowman?" asked Ruth.

Allan almost admonished her for interrupting. As usual, she noticed things that he might have taken for granted. She always seemed to be in tune with God's little details.

Will Bowman said, "Yes, that's right. When Marcus left Joseph's farm, he took the name of Bowman as a sign of thanks. He believed the Bowman family saved his life and sharing their name was a sign of respect and gratefulness. Marcus found his wife in New York City of all places. That's how he became my Great-Great Grandfather. If not for Joseph Bowman, I would not be here today. I owe his family a debt of gratitude that I can never fully repay."

Ben Abrim said, "After this much time, you cannot feel obliged?"

The visitor leaned across the table. He held out his hand and his wife took it in hers. She clasped her hands together and held his hand in her lap. He said, "That's the thing. Up until a few weeks ago, I didn't. I have my wife and son, my mother and some other close family. I didn't give a thought to where I came from or where I was going. God was not big in my life and I kind of felt like the world owed me my big break.

He paused for a drink of water from the small Mason jar that served as a drinking glass in Kinzinger's restaurant.

"I found out that God has a subtle way of telling you when you are wrong. He nudges you onto the path he wants you to follow. It's up to you if you take the hint. Well, my hint came in the form of a seven hundred thousand dollar winning lottery ticket," said Will Bowman.

"That sounds like a lot," said Ruth. Her expression told Allan that she did not really comprehend the amount.

Will continued, "It is. Too much in fact. We bought a house, with one of those smaller houses in the back for my mother. We paid off the cars. We made a big donation to the church that we go to a few times a year. That's where I saw a sign that asked *where is God in your life*? I have been thinking about that for weeks. I figured for me to understand that, I needed to know who I was."

"Which made you ask where you came from?" said Allan. He felt bad for interrupting, but seeing the Lord at work in someone else's life excited him.

"Right," said Will. "That's when I learned the story that Mr. Zook told us. I shared it with Tasha and she pushed me like a good wife does. Together, we traced Joseph Bowman's family halfway across the United States. We have seen so many church districts from Lancaster to Karsten Field. Now, I only have one thing left to do."

Will Bowman reached into his back pocket and pulled out his wallet. Behind the Sears pocket-sized portrait of his family, he removed a rectangular piece of paper. The edges looked slightly tattered. Allan assumed he had been carrying this paper for a long time. Before Will unfolded it, Allan knew what it was. He had seen plenty of cashier's checks at his old real estate job.

Mr. Kinzinger's eyes widened. He said, "That is a check for one hundred thousand dollars."

"We cannot possibly accept that," followed a visibly shaken Ben Abrim.

"Listen," said Will Bowman. "I wanted to give it to the Bowman family. If I have learned anything about the Amish, it is that the whole community is a family. It is the only way I have of repaying Joseph Bowman for saving a man's life."

"Can you excuse us for a moment," said Allan. He gestured for Ben Abrim and Mr. Kinzinger to follow him in the kitchen. On his way out of the dining room, he noticed Ruth introducing the Bowman's to her doll.

In the kitchen, Mr. Kinzinger explained, "Do you realize that money can save Karsten Field? We can buy all the supplies we need for winter and plenty of grain for spring planting. There are a few plows that could stand to be replaced."

Ben Abrim wiped a new patch of sweat from his forehead. He said, "We cannot accept their money. God will provide."

"I think He had a hand in this. This money will defeat our Goliath. How many stones did David take from the stream?" asked Allan.

"Five," answered Ben Abrim, automatically.

Allan asked, "Which did David use to defeat Goliath?"

He seemed to have confused his friend. Ben Abrim said, "What do you mean? It only took one stone."

"Yes, but which stone did he pull from his pouch, the first or the last that he took from the water. God may have chosen a specific stone to defeat the giant, but David did not know which one. I feel that God has chosen this man as our salvation," said Allan.

After a few more minutes of contemplation, Ben Abrim and Mr. Kinzinger agreed. The money would only be used for necessity and the remainder would be put away in case they came into such troubling times again.

Mr. Kinzinger made arrangements for the Bowman's to stay at Troyer's Bed and Breakfast. Ben Abrim invited the new friends to church the next day. All of Karsten Field thanked Will Bowman and his family. Will Bowman thanked them for accepting him and together, they all thanked the Lord.

Karsten Field defeated the drought in an unexpected way. Allan believed God would take care of them. He understood now that it was not *because* they believed, but because God was present in their lives. His plans did not always match human plans and He shows Himself in His own way.

CHAPTER THREE

THE LOST SHEEP

Imagine seeing the world through the eyes of a five-year-old girl.

It must seem like an amazing, wonderfully frightening, awe-inspiring place. So many giant things so far out of reach. At that age, the child has no concept of time, knows only love and has no reason to be scared of the things that keep adults awake at night.

Born on a cold night in January, Ruth Howarth gave her mother very little trouble. Mother Mary's labor lasted only four hours. Father Allan attributed that to not having an epidural as they would have had at an English hospital. Allan suspected his wife kept control of her body through God's grace and without drugs or painkillers to inhibit her. He marveled at Mary's strength both with little Ruth and their older son Benjamin. He knew God had not given men the fortitude to endure such an event. Allan gave thanks for the blessing of his amazing wife and two new children.

Being surrounded by older children, in her family and at the schoolhouse, Ruth started talking at an early age. At five years old, she could speak as well as her seven-year-old brother. Adults, especially Ben Abrim, made it a point to converse with her. Allan also noticed that she talked with herself a lot, like when she played with her doll. Sometimes, he thought she spoke to someone else, but he accredited that to a child's fertile imagination.

Some of the things that made the grown-ups worry did not make much sense to Ruth. She thought they spent too much time worrying about the weather. She knew that either it would rain or it would not. She had more important things to worry about, such as her brother teasing her.

The morning that the rain started, Benjamin climbed out of his bed and jumped onto her bed. He said, "Good morning, thistle hair."

Ruth did not like when her brother called her names. She thought she would never get used to it. She ran her small hand through her frizzy hair, made so by her goose feather pillow.

"You look as wild as the bushes," Benjamin added.

"Mamm!" Ruth wanted the taunting to stop.

Her mother came into the dim room, asking, "What is it little one?"

"Mamm," started Ruth. Then, to make certain she had her mother's attention, she repeated, "Mamm. Benny says I have thistle hair. He says I look like a wild bush."

Ruth knew she could count on the affection and attention of her parents. Like God loved all of his children, she understood that neither Mamm nor Datt liked her better than Benjamin. She knew her parents liked each of their children in different ways.

That morning continued like any other morning. The children enjoyed breakfast with their parents. Mamm would prepare to welcome the schoolchildren and Datt would leave to help at her big sister's house. Ruth liked her sister Alice, even though she was a grown-up. It seemed strange to have a grown-up sister when her brother was so young. Of course, she had a grown-up brother too, but he only came to visit once every thirty years.

At least it seemed that long between Brett's visits. Ruth did not know, nor particularly care to learn to tell time. She believed things happened when God wanted them to, so clocks did not really matter. The only day that did matter to her was her birthday. She often told people, "Tomorrow is my birthday," regardless of the actual date. She knew eventually someone would respond with, "Ja, it is! Another year so soon." Then there would be cake.

Ruth did not ask about her birthday this morning. Today, she wanted only to spend time with her father. He worked very hard and some days she missed him. Some days she needed that good feeling of being held in his arms. She could put her head on his chest and listen to his heartbeat. He would breathe his warm breath on her, causing her own hair to tickle her forehead. Ruth noticed Datt did not hold Alice like that. She was too big. Somehow, Ruth understood that someday she would be too big too.

As Allan tried to leave, Ruth wrapped around his legs, determined to stop him. She begged, "Stay with me."

Her Datt answered, "I have to go help your big sister and Samuel do some chores. I will be back before lunch. We will spend some time together then."

"Promise?" asked Ruth.

"Yes, I promise."

Ruth thought maybe she could get him to stay if she told him, "It's going rain."

Allan looked up at the pale blue sky and said, "It doesn't look like it to me."

Maybe it served as a stall tactic, but Ruth knew it would rain that day. Her imaginary friend sometimes shared things with her. This friend did not always allow her to tell her Mamm and Datt, but sometimes she could. She liked her friend, in his stiff green coat. No one else could see him, but that did not matter to Ruth.

Once Allan had gone, school could begin. The other Karsten children arrived and Mamm would have to teach them. Ruth had another year before she could join Kindergarten, but that did not keep her out of the classroom. Ruth spent most of her time on a small chair next to her mother's desk. She did not have the study responsibilities of the older children, but she pretended to follow along in the various books, always hoping for another picture instead of those pesky words.

Seeing her twin niece and nephew everyday also made school fun. Isaac and Elizabeth, her sister's children, came to school and they could all eat lunch together. Ruth liked being younger than her niece and nephew. They called her Aunt Ruthy. Ruth only heard other grown-ups being called aunt. She was the only aunt-child that she knew.

While Ruth could not tell time, her tummy told her when to eat lunch. Since Datt had promised to be back, Ruth decided on her own to wait outside. She watched the sky turn from blue to gray. She knew the rain would start soon, so she opened her mouth to catch a few drops. She liked the way the drops felt gently splashing on her cheeks and she knew water was good to drink. She felt like it was a special treat from God.

"Careful, a bird might fly over," called her Datt before she saw him.

Happy to see her Datt, she felt an uncontrollable smile grow across her face. She said, "I told you it was going to rain. I was going to save some in a jar for you, if you didn't get back in time."

"Well, I am back in time for lunch," he said. When he came close enough, he did one of her favorite things. He lifted her from the ground in a giant scoop. Her Datt continued, "Besides, I would hardly call this rain."

Ruth hugged him. She believed more rain would be coming and said, "I don't think the hard stuff will come down for a while yet. Are you going to spend some time with me before lunch? You promised."

"I think we should help Mamm with lunch," said Allan. Ruth wanted her Datt to herself today. She did not want to share him with all of the other kids. She learned to share other things, toys, books, but today, she did not want to share her father. Her imaginary friend told her about the rainstorm. The idea reminded her of the story Alice read to her about a man named Noah building a big boat.

In a way, after that, Ruth got her wish. The heavy rains kept her father home for several days. Other than the most necessary things, he did not go out of the house and they did not have the other children for school.

One morning, Ben Abrim and Mr. Menlach came to their house. Ruth sat at the breakfast table, pretending not to listen. She could not help herself when Mr. Menlach said, "It has to stop sometime."

"Not for forty days," Ruth announced, quickly swallowing a bite of scrambled eggs.

She liked Ben Abrim because he always paid attention to her. He treated things she said equally as important to what grown-ups said. He asked, "What would make you say that?"

Ruth wanted to say that her imaginary friend told her, but she felt funny talking about him. She rushed over to her Datt for a little comfort. Then she explained, "Noah has forty days of night in the rain to sail away with the animals."

Maybe she did not get the story quite right. She thought she remembered the important details.

"Gott is gut," said Ben Abrim. "You know of Noah and God's promise."

"Aunt Alice read it to me," Ruth confirmed. She sometimes called her sister *aunt*, as Alice sometimes called her Aunt Ruth when talking to Isaac and Elizabeth.

Ruth's mother, referring to the rain outside, offered, "It may be time to study it again."

Both Ben Abrim and Amos Menlach looked delighted from Ruth's perspective. She guessed they did not expect her to know about things like that.

Mr. Menlach said, "I do not think it will rain for forty days."

A tremendous roar of thunder startled Ruth. She did not like when the thunder and lightning came on so strong. So far, the storm had not been very noisy. She did not mind the rain when it was only rain. The big belch of thunder made Ruth think that Mr. Menlach was wrong and God was telling him so.

Looking out the window, Ben Abrim scratched his head and turned to Allan. He said, "In second thoughts, I will take you up on your offer to check on your children. That distance may be too far for my old frame." He gave an exaggerated wink and held his lower back. Ruth could tell from his hidden smile that he was faking. Still, she did not like the idea of seeing him in pain. Then he added, "Mr. Howarth, perhaps you should consider bringing your family to stay with me until the worst of this storm passes."

Ruth liked that idea. It somehow seemed safer to be up on top of the hill instead of down at the bottom. She waited to see what her father would say.

"Thank you, I will consider it. Now get yourselves home before you get washed away," he said. Ruth understood that he did not want to leave their home yet.

After Ben Abrim and Mr. Menlach left, her Mamm looked worried. She said, "Should we go stay with him?"

"I don't think that will be necessary. He is being overly cautious. Like Mr. Menlach said, it can't rain for forty days. We're not going to float away," said Datt.

Sometimes, Ruth's Mamm had good ideas. She liked when they both agreed on things. Mamm spoke to Datt, "Keep in mind, mein herz, we are at the bottom of the hill and water flows downward."

Allan left then to check on Alice and her family. Ruth waited for him, watching out the window at the seemingly unending rain. She kept breathing on the glass to fog it over and hurriedly draw smiles and flowers before it faded.

And the rain kept coming.

One day, it almost stopped. Almost.

After having no other children around, besides her brother, Ruth enjoyed having Alice and the twins come for lunch. With such a light sprinkle of rain outside, their family walked. Samuel said he did not want to risk getting their buggy stuck on the muddy pass.

"They have been climbing the walls," Alice said to Mary, as they cleaned up after lunch. "They need something to get this energy out of their system."

Ruth's Mamm looked out the window. Her mother said exactly what she hoped, "One day in the rain would not hurt them, I think. What say you, husband?"

Ruth felt tingly. She wanted badly to go outside. She had not been outdoors is such a long time due to the rain. She liked the feel of soft grass on her barefeets and the feel of warm sun. She knew she would not get either of those, but mud squishing between her toes would be a good alternative. She waited with anticipation for her Datt's answer.

Allan said, "Great, let's go play outside."

Isaac led the way, and Ruth took her usual spot at the end of the line. Being the youngest, she almost always went last at every activity. This did not bother her, because her brother, niece and nephew always made sure to include her. Ruth rarely felt left out. Before her Mamm could stop them, the children escaped the house without boots or coats.

Ruth could not remember having so much fun. She danced, slipping in groggy mud puddles. The gentle rain soaked her dress. As she twirled, she watched water spray from the hem in a beautiful fountain. The fun almost ended when Benjamin hit her in the back with a mud ball. He laughed so hard until Isaac splatted him on the forehead with his own mud ball. Ruth did her best to join in, but she did not have very good aim. It surprised her when her father started throwing too.

When Isaac tried to escape one of Benjamin's messiest handfuls, he ran up the hill. He could not stay on his feet and plopped onto his backside. He slid right past Benjamin and stopped with a splash at the bottom of the hill. This seemed like fun to Ruth, and apparently everyone else. Even her Datt wanted a turn.

The fun ended when Mamm came to the bottom of the hill. She ordered, "Mr. Howarth, please come here at this moment."

Her Datt chose to go to Mamm by the seat of his pants. He raced down the hill, spraying mud and water in a fantastic display. Ruth noticed he slid much faster than any of the kids and looked like he would not be able to stop.

The crash of mother and father scared Ruth. She did not want either of them to be hurt and thought they both had to be hurt by the way they tumbled across the yard. When they sat up, her mother looked like she might cry. Then both of her parents started laughing. Ruth knew neither of them got hurt and she started laughing too.

The fun ended with more heavy rain. They filed into the house one at a time to keep from making too much of a mess. Before everyone made it inside, Eli Gundy came running down the hill. Ruth noticed his hard stomping boots splash mud up onto the window. It only lasted a moment as the continuous downpour washed the glass clean.

Eli looked frightened to Ruth. He called loudly to be heard over the weather, "Mr. Howarth, Mr. Menlach, please come. My father needs you."

Allan did not hesitate. He and Samuel left their wives and children. Ruth liked Mr. Gundy's bacon and hoped he would be all right. She watched her father until he was out of sight, which was not far in this curtain of water.

Clean and dry, Ruth waited for her Datt in her favorite spot by the window. She could only see about half way up the hill. She knew he would have to come back down that hill to be with her.

As she watched, heavy flows of mud began to develop. First one stripe covering the grass, and then another. Water, not only from the sky, but also from the river, pushed the mud down the hill, sloshing and bubbling. Watching sticks dance on the surface amused her. Soon, however, the sticks became branches and she could see rocks being pushed by the forceful water. The few small streams suddenly became a flood as wide as the river on the other side of the hill. Ruth watched the water come right up to the house before she ran to her Mamm.

Years later, Ruth would try to think back to that day and that moment. She remembered her Mamm looking very brave. She hurriedly gathered the children with Alice's help, but did not say a word. Ruth trusted her Mamm and waited patiently. She worried that the water might carry away their house, but she did not think her Mamm would allow that.

Ruth's memory told her that her Datt came back. She did not know how long Allan had been gone or what he did when he came back. She could only remember his arms. Those arms, which she associated with God's arms in her prayers, carried her up that hill. It seemed like they were surrounded by water. Even high up, pressed against her Datt's chest, she could feel the flood splashing at her feet. She had an idea that it would be bad if she fell, or if they both fell. Part of her also thought it would be fun to ride the waves back to their house.

She felt her father tremble. She knew they were going to fall. Then Ruth looked to the top of the hill and saw her imaginary friend. He looked perfectly dry, his green jacket crisp and not a drop on his funny soup bowl hat. The moment before Allan lost his footing, her friend smiled at them. She did not think her Datt saw it, but he suddenly gained strength and made his way to the safety at the top of the hill.

As usual, Ruth's imaginary friend protected as he promised. He led them safely to Ben Abrim's house and even pushed back some of the rain to make it easier. With all of the people and commotion, Ruth did not get a chance to ask her father if he saw her friend helping them. Ruth's mind went on to other things. As she snuggled with her father that night, she remembered something more important. She said to her Datt, "You finally get to spend some time with me."

After the flood, it seemed strange to Ruth that they did not have any rain for so long. It kept getting hotter outside. It made her glad that her imaginary friend came to visit more often when she had less to keep her occupied. Her Mamm and Datt would not let her and Benny play outside on these really hot days. In the mornings, when she woke up before her brother, Ruth would talk with her imaginary friend. Mostly, he would tell her how wonderful God is and that he wanted to keep her safe.

Some days they shared a laugh when her Datt stood outside her bedroom door. Allan always thought Ruth talked to her doll, but he did not know about her friend. Her friend would disappear right before her Datt came into the room. She loved seeing her father first thing in the morning and would forget about her protector. Since helping her during the flood, she thought of her friend as a protector. Her Mamm would have called him a guardian angel, she guessed.

Allan did not leave as early as usual to go fishing this Saturday, so Ruth asked if she could join him. Naturally, Benjamin wanted to be included. He asked to carry their Datt's fishing pole, which left Ruth with the heavy bucket.

Determined to be helpful, she offered to carry it despite barely being able to wrap her arms around it. She knew she could not lift it once it was full of water.

Ben Abrim sidetracked them on the way to the river. Ruth did not like how he looked when he talked about needing food and dying crops. She thought something might be wrong, but her Datt did not act like it. If he did not worry, then neither would she. She felt some more relief when he said, "Why don't you and your brother take our things down by the river? I will follow you in a moment."

On their way to the river, Ruth liked to cross over the new bridge that Mr. Esch built after the flood. Benjamin preferred going under it. He had enough space to go in the low side crouching, but he came out on hands and knees at the top of the hill. Their mother warned him that spiders could be under there. Ruth thought that was exactly why he went that way.

This summer, the river looked a lot different than she remembered. She and Benny had more shallow water to play in and where it was deep enough, it did not flow as fast. Her brother always searched for frogs or little black snakes. Ruth liked snakes about as much as her father and that was not at all. The boy and his reptile friends could be quite frightening. Ruth gave thanks that the heat and low water kept the creatures hidden.

While they waited for their father, it seemed like a good idea to splash each other to keep cool. Of course, neither Ruth nor Benjamin worried about throwing up mud with their splashes. They had a few minutes of fun, until Benjamin thought he spied a frog and followed it down the dry bank a few feet. This left Ruth alone to watch the cool water trickle over her small toes. She watched her feet through a magic mirror of water shimmering in the morning sun.

Then something caught her eye. In the sediment of gray and brown rocks, she saw five very different stones. Smooth, round and yellow, they seemed very important to her. Adults do not always understand why or what makes certain things more important than others. Adults have their own value system and concerns. Sometimes, to a child, something is important simply because it is. Ruth gathered the small stones in one hand and waited to show them to her father.

"What are those for, mein herz?" her father asked, after they prayed together. Sometimes, Allan would hold his children and pray for no apparent reason that Ruth could see.

She explained the stones to her Datt the way she imagined them. She said, "This one is for Mamm and Datt. This one is Benjamin and me. Here is Alice, Samuel, Isaac and Elizabeth. This one is for Ben Abrim. And this is everyone else in Karsten Field."

"Aren't you forgetting someone?" asked her father.

She knew she was not, but recounted everyone in her head to make sure. When she could not think of anyone else, she asked "Who?"

Allan asked, "Which one is God?"

The answer seemed obvious to Ruth. Sometimes, her Datt and other adults could not see things that she could see clearly. It amused her when they did not understand. She said, "God's not a little rock, silly. He's the river."

She could tell her Datt liked the idea of the stones. Ruth noticed he got dreamy, as she called it, after she told him God was the river. It made sense to her that a great big God would carry all of them like the river moved the small stones and pebbles.

They left the river without catching a single fish. That did not bother Ruth too much. She preferred to watch the shiny animals swim to the taste of them on her plate. Ruth really did not like eating animals because she always imagined their cuddly faces. Still, she knew her Mamm worked hard, so she did not complain about the food blessed from the Lord.

When it came time for a nap after lunch, the bee fluttering by her open window made Ruth want to be someplace else. She wanted to be outside with the bee, gathering flowers. She knew the hot weather was killing the flowers. It also made it hard to sleep during naptime. Even with a slight breeze, she could not get comfortable. Her father came in to give her a kiss and said he was going to Mr. Kinzinger's restaurant.

Mrs. Kinzinger made extra sweet lemonade and she did not want to miss that on such a hot day. "May I please go with you, Datt?"

Ruth learned quickly that when she gave her father a certain look, the answer would always be *yes.* She curved her mouth down slightly and opened her eyes as wide as she could. He once called the look a *puppy dog face.*

Kinzinger's restaurant seemed like a different world to Ruth. They had electricity for one thing. Electricity meant cold air in the summer and warm air in the winter. Her Datt told her it was to make outsiders feel comfortable when they came to visit. Ruth usually did not get to come to the restaurant or any of the shops when they were busy with outsiders.

Ruth once asked her Mamm why they stayed away from the outsiders. Her Mamm explained, "A good shepherd does not allow his sheep to mix with wolves. You, my little lamb, I do not want to get eaten."

She thought her mother meant that the outsiders were like wolves, which made them bad. Ruth did not think all outsiders were bad. She guessed there were other good sheep in the world. It seemed too big not to be true.

When the strangers arrived, the thought of lost sheep made Ruth curious instead of afraid of hungry wolves.

Their very different appearance interested Ruth more than anything else. She never saw anyone with such dark skin. Her father and the other Karsten men got darker skin in the summer, but it faded over the winter. This family had dark brown skin and it amazed her.

She asked her father what made them so dark, but Ben Abrim answered. He said, "My dear, the good Lord paints his children in all the colors of the rainbow."

Already at her age, Ruth had ideas about how God made babies. She imagined a big room made of clouds where He sat and watched the angels work. In her mind, they took great care picking out hair and eyes, putting all the pieces together like her mother put together her doll. Now, she had to rethink it somewhat. It did not seem like a cloth doll could be easily painted. She decided the angels made babies of something else that God could paint. She watched her father help paint several houses and decided they must use wooden dolls. She did not think God was as sloppy when it came to painting as her father was. Her Datt always splattered some in his hair and all over the ground.

The grown-ups told a story about David and Goliath and how some outsiders hurt other outsiders. This made Ruth think of the wolves again. Pie and lemonade made the story seem a little less scary.

The stranger had a piece of paper that made her father, Ben Abrim and Mr. Kinzinger very excited. When they went off to talk about it, Ruth decided to show her doll to the boy named Chris. He was older than she was, and despite looking so different, seemed very nice. Ruth thought maybe his mother called him a little lamb too.

Something changed with that meeting. Ruth understood that. Whatever worried Ben Abrim disappeared after the strangers left. They stayed for church, but Ruth wished they could have stayed a little longer. She loved everyone in

Karsten Field, but she also had the idea that she wanted to meet more people. Her Mamm may have warned her against wolves, but her imaginary friend told her that God filled the world with wonderful people too.

After that, the weather changed too. It took several weeks, or months, Ruth could not tell for sure, but it started to cool. Her father spent more time on outdoor chores. One day, she listened to Ben Abrim discussing a trip with her Datt. She liked the idea of a trip. It made her wonder what far off places in the outside world might be like. Ruth had a way of listening to grown-ups that seemed like she was not listening. They did not include her in the talk, but she did not always understand them either. Sometimes, she had questions and that gave her away.

"Mr. Kinzinger has told me of an auction this Saturday. They are holding it at the county fairgrounds to draw a larger crowd," said Ben Abrim. Ruth loved to see the old man smile. Today, he seemed to have an even bigger grin.

Allan deliberately dropped the stack of shingles he was carrying. Ruth wondered why he always had to be mending the roof. She noticed he spent as much time up there as he did on any other chore. She never noticed a leaky roof in the schoolhouse.

Her father wiped his brow with an old, wrinkled handkerchief. It used to be white, but now looked mostly dull yellow to Ruth. He responded to Ben Abrim, "What do you hope to find at this auction, Mr. Zook?"

Ben Abrim took a quick step to move next to Allan and the two of them started to walk around the side of the house. Ruth got up from her spot in the dirt and followed after them, skipping.

"I propose we take some of the extra money and buy the needed equipment we have discussed," said Ben Abrim.

Her father stopped suddenly and Ruth almost skipped into him. He put a hand on her shoulder and she looked up smiling. Allan gave her a brief smile and turned back to Ben Abrim. He said, "If you are asking me, I say our first priority is to make sure we have plenty of food for winter and we are prepared for spring planting. I don't know of anybody's plow that needs more than a few bolts tightened. Isn't the money better left in case of some other catastrophe?"

Ben Abrim said, "I do not advocate taking all of it. Do not think I meant we go on a spend spree like young men on a rumspringa. I only mean that Mr. Esch and Mr. Gundy could both use new blades for their respective work. Mr. Kurtz and Mr. Otto have both mentioned the need for new cultivators. And, of all things, Mr. Lenaxel has a cracked axel on his big wagon. This would by no means be a frivolous trip."

It looked to Ruth that Ben Abrim had convinced her father. Her Datt wiped his forehead for a second time. This usually meant he had surrendered to whatever proposal had come his way, be it from her Mamm, herself, her brother or Ben Abrim. She took the quiet opportunity between the two men to ask if she could go.

"I would like to go on a trip," Ruth said.

"Would you now, my little lamb?" said Allan. She liked it better when he called her *his heart*. *Little Lamb* belonged to her mother.

The idea seemed fantastic to her. Ruth had no idea what an *ox son* was, but the way Ben Abrim described it made her want to go. It sounded like they would find everything they ever needed there.

"Well, Mr. Zook, I think we have no choice. If mein herz wants to go, then we go," said Allan. "But, I have one question. If Mr. Lenaxel's wagon cannot make the trip, then how are we going to bring back our purchases?"

Ben Abrim's smile got bigger, if that was possible. He said, "Mr. Kinzinger has an English friend that will carry us there and back in his Tundra truck."

If Ruth thought she was excited before, on Saturday, she became doubly excited. Benjamin chose to go to the Menlachs to play with Michael and Dolph. They were a little older, but he did his best to keep up with them. Not only would Ruth have her Datt all to herself, she would be taking her first ride in a truck. She watched the English automobiles come and go from the shops and Mr. Kinzinger's restaurant, but she had never been inside one.

The *Tundra truck*, as Ben Abrim called it, stood taller than any of their buggies. She did not know why it was called *Tundra*, but Ben Abrim explained it had to do with the people that built it. Shiny black reflected all over the outside and tan leather covered the seats inside, as smooth as Samuel and Alice's buggy.

Mr. Kinzinger's English friend, called Phil, opened the wide back door for her. Ruth needed a hand scrambling up into the truck. It had a special step on the side, but she was not quite tall enough. The back seat had more than plenty of room for her, her Datt and Ben Abrim. She wanted to bounce on the soft seats, but her father stopped her right before she started. He sat by the window and Ben Abrim boxed her in on the other side. Phil reminded them to put on seatbelts and Allan showed her how to click hers into place. The tightness across her lap did not squash her excitement at all.

Once Mr. Kinzinger climbed into the front passenger seat, Phil turned on the ignition. The truck roared and Ruth could feel her seat vibrate. An assortment of lights and dinging sounds burst from the front. Loud, peculiar music seemed to squeal from the doors and under the seats. Phil hurriedly pushed a button and the music vanished. Then he pushed another button, this one on the door, and all of the side windows dropped down with a low hum. The quite *vrrrrr* came from behind as well. Ruth twisted around to see the wide back window dip out of sight. Then the truck began to move.

The world passed by faster than Ruth could watch. Things like trees and other cars turned into blurs. She would have been scared, if not for being so thrilled. The wind whipped through the cabin of the truck sending her brown hair into a frenzy.

This brought on the giggles. The truck ride ended much sooner than she would have liked.

Phil stopped them in a field with hundreds of other cars. Ruth guessed there had to be hundreds because she did not know a bigger number. All of the people seemed to be going to several huge barns. They did not look much different from Karsten barns, except they were larger and made of metal. Some had rows of tall windows. People paraded cows and horses out of one of the huge open doors.

Inside, the building seemed unbelievably large. It stretched as far as Ruth could see. Rows of people and tables ran off in both directions. Down one aisle, she could see stacks of cages holding roosters and hens. They clucked a greeting to her. Down the next aisle, she spotted quilts and clothes. Somewhere, over the smell of chickens and cows, she could smell apple pie.

This world amazed her.

Ruth followed along behind her father, trying to keep up in the crowd. Everyone else there seemed as excited as she was. They barely paid attention to her as they pushed from table to table.

She had to stop at one table. Someone carved candles to look like small tree trunks, except they had faces. Two of the candles had been burning a while and the flame chased the wick down into the body of the candle. From there, it flashed out through glass marble eyes making the candle seem alive. Ruth stared into the puzzling face for what felt like a long time. When she looked up, she could not see her father anywhere.

Amidst the bustle of the buyers and sellers, Ruth did not recognize a single face. She knew she had to catch up to her Datt, so she started in the same direction they had been going. Pushing out of the narrow aisle, she came to a wide intersection. With three choices, Ruth did not know which way to go. She could not see her Datt, Ben Abrim, Mr. Kinzinger or Phil. And no one seemed to see her. One woman, twice as wide as Mrs. Menlach, almost stepped on her. Ruth moved over to a corner table to avoid being trampled by these outsiders. That made her think of the wolves again and she started to get scared.

With tears pooling in the corners of her eyes, Ruth turned to look at the long table pressing against her back. The owner took the time to spread a nice cover over the table. From where Ruth stood, she could see the rusty metal table legs behind the colorful pattern of the tablecloth. A variety of paintings lay across the table or stood on small display stands. Through the tears in her eyes, she thought these paintings looked familiar.

One looked like the Fencil's house. Another reminded her of Mr. Gundy's pigsty. The one closest to her could have been the very schoolhouse where she spent most of her time. The woman behind the table did not look like anyone she knew from Karsten Field. She could hear the woman talking to an older couple.

"My grandfather painted these, but we need the money," she said.

Before Ruth could hear more, another voice caused her to spin around suddenly.

"I had a friend that liked to paint," said Ruth's imaginary friend. She could see him plainly, dressed in his usual green jacket. Ruth would not have wanted to wear that heavy coat. The warmth of the building already added to her uneasy state. No one else seemed to notice her friend. He continued, "Have you gotten yourself lost?"

Ruth nodded vigorously and a tear drop fell to the smooth concrete floor, turning the dust at the edge of the table into a tiny mud puddle.

"Do you trust me?" asked Ruth's friend.

She nodded again.

"As God is my father, I follow him. So now, you must follow me," said her friend. He turned and started walking. No one moved out of his way or begged his pardon. Ruth almost thought it looked like he walked through some people. She did her best to keep up, always watching for that green jacket and funny metal bowl on his head.

Allan carried the canvas bag holding five thousand dollars cash. He somehow had been elected to hold the money and it made him feel extremely uncomfortable. He had not been to an auction in a few years, so he felt wary. He kept a watchful eye on anybody that came too close to him or the bag.

Of course, he realized if someone were to rob him, then God had other uses for the money. The busy vendors and shouting auctioneers did not help him relax. He pushed through the crowd behind Mr. Kinzinger and his English friend. Ben Abrim and Ruth trailed after him.

Phil stopped for a moment by a booth selling candles. He saw someone he knew and they exchanged a few words. That did not slow Ben Abrim or Mr. Kinzinger. Allan politely waited for Phil, but he wanted to get the money to its destination by the large farm equipment in the back of the building.

Allan checked once to make sure Ruth still followed him, then Ben Abrim pulled him by the arm. He wanted to show Allan a set of carving knives that he thought would be ideal for Mr. Gundy.

Finally, clearing the throng of shoppers and lookee-loos, they made it back to the business area. A small group of Mennonite men stood in front of a row of horse pulled cultivators. They looked ready to haggle. Mr. Kinzinger and his friend Phil went to work on them. Once they reached an agreeable price, they called Allan over for the money.

Allan set the bag down on a convenient table, relieved to be parting with it. With his hands free of responsibility, something struck him as odd. He suddenly realized another responsibility that had fallen from the front of his mind.

He looked around for Ruth. Usually, she would be at either his left or right heel, waiting patiently for his attention. He admired her patience, which had to be greater than anyone else he knew. However, he did not find her at his side at this moment. His heartbeat quickened as he scanned the crowd.

Not as many people waded through the large equipment area and Allan could easily tell she was not in sight. That meant she had been separated back by the craft tables. His chest tightened and his breath seemed to get more difficult to draw in. They enjoyed so much freedom and peace in Karsten Field that Allan neglected to warn Ruth of common troubles that the Englishers face and often cause. Anyone could have carried or coaxed her away for any reason.

Allan felt a burst of fear and anger almost overtake him. He stepped away from the table.

"Allan, the money..." started Ben Abrim. He must have realized what was wrong and stopped mid-sentence.

"Means nothing if I don't find my daughter," Allan finished.

As he headed into the sea of people, Allan said a prayer to himself.

"Father, I ask you to place your shield around my wayward sheep. Bring her back into the fold that she may continue to praise you."

As if in answer to his prayer, the crowd seemed to thin. It reminded Allan of the book of Exodus. He knew he was no Moses, but the uncontrollable sea of people parted before him. At the end of the row, not twenty feet from him, Ruth waited patiently. She stood with a smile on her face, admiring some caged rabbits under a bright red "For Sale" sign. Allan would happily buy her all of the rabbits, knowing that she was not lost.

"Where did you wander off to?" Allan asked. He hugged her and realized it was probably too hard for her small frame. She winced, but he saw a look of relief in her eyes.

"You were right there and then you were gone," said Ruth.

Allan took her by her tiny hand and led her back to the others. He saw Phil talking to a man in a security uniform. The Englisher seemed like a good man, willing to help no matter the cause. Ben Abrim slowly knelt to Ruth's height.

The old man said, "This place is so big. After all that has beset us this year, my heart could not stand losing you."

Ruth faced Ben Abrim with an innocent expression. Allan could not bear to let go of his daughter's hand, but she pulled free to explain. She pointed down the long center aisle.

"Isaac led me through there," she said.

"Your nephew?" asked Allan. He knew for certain that Alice kept her children home; otherwise, they would have travelled together.

"No, my friend Isaac. He said he would always watch out for me," said Ruth. She had that tone in her voice like when only she understood something that should be easy to understand. He expected her to call him *silly* again.

The talk of a strange friend always watching his daughter made Allan somewhat uneasy. He asked, "Where is this Isaac now?"

"He comes and goes," said Ruth.

Ben Abrim used Allan's arm to pull himself to a standing position. He looked to Allan like he might know Ruth's friend. He had a way with Ruth that caused them to get along better than other adults and young children.

Ben Abrim asked, "Does your friend wear a nice green coat, maybe with a colored ribbon on it?"

Ruth nodded. She said, "He also has a funny hat. It is round like yours but made of metal."

Ben Abrim leaned close to Allan, "It sounds like she is describing a young soldier I once told you about."

It did seem that way, thought Allan. He remembered, years ago, that Ben Abrim told him the story of how Karsten Field came to be. He remembered Mr. Karsten's son, Isaac, left to fight in World War I against their beliefs and his father's wishes. His return from Europe predated a telegram marking the boy's death six weeks earlier. Ben Abrim never offered an explanation why the people of Karsten Field, then called Thuisland, made claims of seeing young Isaac only days before the telegram arrived.

Now, Allan thought, Ruth had a guardian angel.

CHAPTER FOUR

LIFE ON CANVAS

The house felt strangely empty.

Margaret could not understand how one man could take up so much space. Now that he was gone, he left a void. They bought a three-bedroom house years ago, in anticipation of children that never came. Having it paid off in the early eighties, they never found reason to move.

Even during the sickness, they kept the house.

Margaret did not need it any more.

Her husband, Stephen, took care of everything. His job paid the bills and provided friends. Margaret stayed home. One of the bedrooms became her sewing room. The other unused room became his computer room. They filled the house with things, but never really became attached to them.

Stephen took care of everything, except the medical bills. The prolonged stays at the hospital accumulated. Since retiring, the insurance did not cover what it used to. The Life insurance covered even less. By the time Margaret signed the last check for the funeral home, she had no money left and close to one hundred thousand dollars in bills from the hospital.

When things went bad, she did not want Stephen to suffer. He took care of her his whole life. Margaret wanted desperately to make him comfortable in his final days. She approved home health visits and rehab stays that she knew Stephen would never have said yes to. The numbers kept adding up and Margaret did not know how to pay for them.

She looked around the house again. The nook where they shared their morning coffee together looked uninviting. His computer and LCD TV had already been sold. The movers would be coming in a week. She planned an estate sale for Monday. Most of their furniture would not fit in her new, smaller place.

The sale of the house would cover the bills. However, in this economy, the real estate agent told her it could take months to get a buyer. Margaret decided to sell most everything else so she could put a few months back for rent. After that, she would probably look for a part-time job at Wal-Mart or Hy-Vee.

Walking the halls, Margaret looked at the faded rectangular outlines on the old wallpaper. Pictures of their trips to Hawaii, Canada and Europe lined those walls for too many years. Bringing on the next bout of tears, she wished the walls had been covered with pictures of children and grandchildren. It would have been easier to share the loss. She got a few sympathy cards and the neighbors brought a couple meals. Still, Margaret felt like no one cared. They all had troubles of their own.

She felt like she had no one to turn to.

Getting ready for the yard sale, Margaret remembered the attic. She had not been up there in years. It completely slipped her mind, as if she had nothing else on it. She managed to snag the short cord dangling from the ceiling by standing on a chair. She almost lost her balance. Stephen would have chided her for that. He always protected her.

The stairs unfolded, swinging down from the ceiling. The springs made that horrible squeaking noise, like a creature growling for being disturbed from a long slumber. Then that black opening waited for her. She thought she remembered the location of the pull string for the only hundred-watt bulb up there. Other than that, she had no idea what Stephen kept up there.

The light blinked on with a click as she pulled the string. The strong glare caused her to cover her eyes for a moment. Then, she carefully made her way along the narrow plywood walkway. The original builder never intended for the attic to be a storage place. Stephen added the retractable stairs and plywood walkways a couple years after they signed the papers. Margaret loved how handy he was. Her husband could solve any problem they faced. She worried how she would do that on her own.

In the first boxes, she found some old ties and sports coats with hideously wide lapels. Not that she was a fashion guru, but Margaret could not understand how they had such poor taste back in the seventies. Her husband must have abandoned the diagonal stripes on these ties years ago.

Another box held some of her mother's possessions. As an only child, Margaret had been close to both of her parents. Naturally, she kept their wedding silver and a few other mementos. This box sat on top of one filled with family photos from her childhood. If Margaret started going through these, she knew she would spend the rest of the day up here.

She moved along, carefully ducking under the angled rafters, watching her feet on the plywood spanning the joists. If she stepped off, her foot would go right through the itchy fiberglass insulation. She did not think the sheetrock would hold her weight, even though she weighed less than one thirty these days.

Weight had always been a challenge for her. Stephen never seemed to mind, but Margaret wondered if that did not contribute to their lack of children. Both of them passed fertility tests. It always seemed like something else got in the way. Big vacation plans. Extra hours for the next promotion. The weather: too hot or too cold. Then, one day, they were too old. Stephen decided when that day was.

So, no son or daughter to go up in the attic for her. No one to help her if she got her foot stuck, punching it through the ceiling beneath her.

Margaret had a worse thought. What if she did not stop with her foot? What if her whole body crashed through to the hall below? By now, she had to be over the bannister. She pictured herself hitting the rail and tumbling to the first floor.

Stephen would not approve.

Margaret shook off the thought and looked about the rest of the attic. Stephen mostly filled this area with stuff they no longer wanted or needed.

"Why would anybody else want this stuff?" she asked out loud.

The sound of her voice surprised her in the all-consuming quiet. She had spoken very little since the funeral. She had passing words with a few visitors, but not much. She and Stephen had their own silent language. She did not have much use for words, especially now that he was gone.

The thought of people rooting through their old junk gave her a sickly depressive feeling. If Stephen had decided they did not need it, it made sense that no one else would have a use for it either. Margaret decided to give up her search.

Ready to head back downstairs, she caught sight of a dingy canvas sheet in the far corner. Behind all of the other boxes, it had to be one of the first things Stephen put up here, decades ago.

This far from the wobbly spring staircase, the air became stale. The A/C dissipated long before it could reach this far. Margaret felt a little sweat form behind her ears. It seemed unlady-like to sweat and she wanted this experience to be over quickly. Whatever Stephen put under that canvas, it straddled two joists. It did not even merit the worth to rest on solid plywood. Margaret knelt at the edge of the plywood and reached out for it. The thought of falling flashed through her head again. She guessed she had to be over her sewing room, close to the side of the house. The fall would not be as bad, but she increased her chance of landing on her needles or her good scissors.

The large attic vent gave her some relief from the stale air. Daylight crept in through the wide slats. If that old light bulb quit on her, she did not think it would be enough light to see her way back downstairs.

"Come here you," she said to the canvas. Margaret stretched and did not fall. She would not be looking at her house from a new angle today. She pulled the sheet back and found something she never expected.

It looked like a stack of oil paintings. She could only see the one on top, framed in plain rough cedar. It seemed simple enough. It showed a house on a hill surrounded by green grass and trees back in the distance. It was a country scene with no other landmarks. Underneath it, Margaret could see the edges of five more frames. Stephen never expressed his feelings about painted art. They did not have any hanging on their walls. Art to him was a well-executed football play.

Margaret struggled with the stack getting it downstairs. In the end, she made three separate trips, two frames each time. She got all of the paintings to the kitchen counter and had to take a break. Her lungs did not sustain her like they used to. After two flights of stairs, including the folding attic ones, she went to lie down on the couch.

Her exhaustion outmatched her curiosity for the moment. She wanted to study the paintings, to know where they came from, but a nap came first. Margaret knew they would be there in an hour, if they had been there thirty years.

A strange dream disrupted her nap. She saw her husband, but he looked like he did back in college. He still had the athlete's physique, although the high school injury kept him from playing college football. Margaret did not know Stephen in college. They met right after, so she never knew his interests and hobbies of that time.

In her dream world, Stephen had a particular hobby. She found him in a large, sunlit room. High skylights had been pulled open from a chain and pulley system on the wall. The huge glass panels let in a calming breeze that ruffled the white curtains hanging around the room.

Margaret thought the room looked pristine, until she saw the red droplets on the floor. The splatters made a trail through the curtains, until a footprint smeared the sanguine path. Behind the next curtain, yellow drops mixed with the red. Soon, she found other colors in large puddles across the floor. The white curtains now held a full palette of streaks and the occasional handprint.

The initial purity of the room gave way to chaos at the center. Margaret discovered a man she almost did not recognize. Every color of oil paint stained his loose-fitting clothes. A black glob of the paint started under his nose and streaked down his right cheek like a misshapen moustache.

He held a long brush like a sword or magic wand pointed at a defenseless easel. Margaret gasped when she saw his work in progress. She had seen it before, in the waking world. She saw it on top of the stack she found in the attic. It looked exactly the same. The same house, or was it a cabin?

"You painted these?" Margaret asked.

Stephen smiled at her. She missed that smile dearly. He gave no other answer before her eyes fluttered open from her nap.

Margaret moved to the kitchen as fast as her old joints allowed. She unstacked the paintings and leaned them up against the backsplash tile, side-by-side. She moved deliberately, but could not deride the urgent feeling in her heart. If Stephen had painted these, it would be her last connection to him. Something tangible that he created, not some photo on a beach.

She had nothing else left. She sacrificed everything.

Margaret stared at the paintings for a long time. She moved around her kitchen to get the best view of each one. She traced the brush strokes with her fingertips. Old dry paint flaked when her fingernails rubbed too close. She would never forget these paintings for the rest of her life.

She studied the first one, the cabin on a hill. It was not a traditional cabin with large Lincoln Log stacked corners. It looked more like the house from that old TV show, Little House on the Prairie. It had a nice porch across the front, but no second story. Trees lined the house on the right and more trees stood behind in the distance. There seemed to be some large fields sloping away from the back of the house. A worn dirt path led off the canvas to the left.

Margaret wondered where that path went. She guessed from the second painting that it went to a huge barn. She rearranged the pictures so that the barn stood to the left of the cabin. The paths matched almost exactly, like putting together a giant jigsaw puzzle. The path from the cabin had to be the same path in the painting of the barn. From the coloring on the trees, she guessed they were painted at different times of the year. Despite the slight seasonal difference, Margaret believed they belonged together.

The next one looked a little different. If these places existed anywhere other than her husband's imagination, then they were probably close because the trees looked the same. However, she did not think this setting was next to the first two. She did not see a connecting path or any similar landmarks. A long white building, which made her think of a schoolhouse with a regular house attached to it, rested in a low area. Margaret thought that maybe it sat at the bottom of a hill.

She wished Stephen had signed his name on these. Instead, he only scrawled an *S* in the bottom right corner of each. Margaret believed her husband painted the pictures, but seeing his name would have made it more real for her. It stirred up plenty of emotion as it was.

The next two did not leave as much of an impression on her. They definitely belonged in the group, but Margaret did not feel the same connection. One, of a nice two-story house, seemed a little more modern than the cabin. The other looked like a farmhouse with a huge pigpen on the back left side. Neither of these showed any people, but the pigs in the pen looked back at her with almost child-like expressions.

The final piece of art did not show a building or anything. It was a landscape with more of those beautiful fields. This picture overflowed with yellows, whites and golds. It looked like a country harvest, but the ground almost blended with the sky in brightness. An amazing sunset washed out the hints of blue sky. Trees stood at either side of the field like onlookers at the Thanksgiving Day parade.

A figure in the center caught Margaret's attention. It looked like a man, but it was so far in the background of the painting that she could barely tell. The shape and darker color of the figure gave her that impression though. Another impression it left on her was that the man was being lifted up from the ground.

When she finally saw it, Margaret wept. The revelation of the painting moved her in a way she had not expected. She saw it in the folds of the clouds, in the shadowed lines caused by the sun, in the rows of cut wheat.

An angel.

It had to be.

The angel lifted the man from the ground. It seemed so obvious now, through her tears. Only moments before, it had been completely hidden in the complexity of the brush strokes.

At one time, her Stephen had been capable of that kind of passion. Maybe he had not shown it in these last years, but she remembered it. She remembered his touch. She cried for the stranger in that painting. She cried for her lost husband. She believed in her heart and prayed every night that the angels carried her Stephen to be with God.

In Margaret's sleepless nights, she thought a lot about that. Her husband never fully embraced her beliefs. He delivered her to church every Sunday, but never stayed. She worried that they might not be together when her time came.

Somehow, this painting made her feel that they would.

The ringing phone interrupted Margaret's thoughts. She moved across the kitchen, wiping her cheeks, not realizing she smeared make-up on her white blouse as she lowered her hand.

"Hello," she said, trying to hide the waver in her voice. She cried a lot these past few weeks, but she did not want the world to know it.

"Margaret, sorry to bother you. I have some bad news."

It was the probate lawyer. She could not remember his name, but he always called with bad news. She suspected he knew no other kind. One of Stephens's old co-workers gave her number to the lawyer. She did not think she needed him though. Her husband had a will, although they had nothing and no one to leave it to. On the contrary, he seemed to need her and his bills always seemed to be on the top of the stack.

Margaret did not think her heart could take any more bad news. It took tremendous will for her to ask, "What is the news?"

"We found another medical bill," he said.

"But I thought you had all of Stephen's bills," she started.

He never seemed to show emotion and never waited for her to express herself. He said, "Not your husband's. Did you have surgery about three years ago?"

She did. She had breast cancer. By God's grace, she was a survivor. She wished this man did not know all of her personal details. She mumbled, "Yes, I did."

"Were you not aware that insurance did not cover all of those expenses? You have six hundred fourteen dollars and sixty-eight cents in collections."

"Thank you for telling me," Margaret said. She hung up the phone without checking to see if the conversation had ended.

Another bill. More money that she did not have. What else could they take from her? Where would she get the money?

Six hundred dollars.

The answer wrenched her heart.

Six paintings.

What if she could sell the paintings for a hundred dollars each, Margaret thought. The probate lawyer did not know about the paintings, so she could do with them as she pleased. Then she would have the money, but she would also have nothing left of her husband. Maybe she did not know God well enough, but she did not think He would ask her to give up everything.

"Would You ask that of me?" she said to the empty kitchen.

No one responded. Margaret did not expect an answer. She almost made herself smile to fight off the next bout of tears. She envisioned God speaking to her, his booming voice rattling the cabinets, coffee cups swinging on their hooks. Like in the movies, he would sound like Morgan Freeman and he would have all the answers.

The smile faded. Margaret did not have any answers. She knew God did not talk to people, at least not in a way that could be heard with human ears. She thought maybe He sent her a message by guiding her to the paintings. She wanted badly to hold on to a piece of her husband, especially something like this that came from his heart and hands.

Margaret wondered, how cruel was God to take Stephen, her husband and only friend, and then snatch away this last piece of him too.

She prayed, "Dear Father, I'm not sixty-five yet, so I hope I still have some years left. If you have time for me, I need a sign. If You are taking away all my happiness, where will I find peace?"

Margaret stood, silently, in the middle of her kitchen for a while longer. She could do little else but stare at the paintings. Her grief pummeled her like those heavyweight boxers Stephen used to watch. With great sobs, she stumbled toward the counter for support. Margaret's hands slid across the marble countertop and she let her forehead drop to the cold surface. She almost did not notice the newspaper she knocked to the floor.

After a few minutes of letting the marble cool her burning face, Margaret tried to compose herself. She looked around as if someone might have been watching. She saw nothing, except the fake wood paneling of the dining room through the kitchen arch.

The house could not be left a mess, so Margaret knelt to pick up the paper scattered over the floor. The advertisement on the back page caught her eye. It gave her two ideas simultaneously. First, she probably never would have seen it if she had not accidently knocked it to the floor after praying. Secondly, it told her what needed to be done.

County Fair Auction – One Weekend Only. Vendors wanted. $25 a table, in air conditioning.

That would be the perfect place to sell the paintings, Margaret thought. She hoped it would not be too late to get a table. The newspaper had been sitting on her counter for two weeks. Stephen was not there to read them any longer.

On the day of the sale, Margaret curled her hair. Maybe it was a little thin and not nearly as blonde as it used to be, but at least it was all hers. She had no intention of getting a wig. It worked for some, but not for her. She had her mother's narrow cheekbones. Stephen used to say her mother had a hatchet face. He never said it about her, but Margaret knew she looked a lot like her mother. She remembered her mother did the wig thing near the end. It did not work with the shape of her face. Margaret hated to admit it to herself, but her mother looked like a dried up tree with a beehive stuck in its top branches.

Margaret did not want to put a beehive on her head.

She came to the fairgrounds early, with her curled hair and light blue pantsuit. She intended to be early and thought seven o'clock was. Some men, she thought might be Amish, already had their tables set. At the back of the long warehouse-type building, some others lined up various farm equipment. From the looks of their displays, these men had been here for hours.

"So much for being early," Margaret said to herself.

She looked at her table on Row J, number 316. She managed to get the last one. That is what the promoter said anyway. He told her that she got lucky and he would give her a discount if she would sign up for the next three shows, including one on the other side of the state in Sioux City. Margaret only wanted the one show. She only needed one. After that, it would be too late for her. She wondered how many other *lucky* people got the same offer.

Scuffed yellow tape marked the boundaries of her booth. She had one six-foot folding table to hold everything she brought with her. She decided to bring a few other things that might pass as antiques: her old teapot, her mother's cast-iron skillet. The main thing she hoped was to sell those paintings. If she could make at least that six hundred dollars today, she could move into her new place with clear credit, if nothing else.

She ended up with the corner spot on one of the main aisles. Supposedly, the original seller backed out at the last moment. This seemed to be a prime spot. Margaret felt sure she would sell her paintings.

Two hours later, she had not sold a single thing. She tried to stand a few of the paintings. The others laid flat over the tablecloth she brought from home. It did not fit the table, so she kept adjusting it. First, it would be too short on the front and then too short on the back. Some of the other tables had no coverings at all. Margaret wanted hers to look at least somewhat attractive, maybe draw someone with enough money to get all six paintings at once.

As the crowd thickened throughout the day, Margaret started to feel desperate. No one seemed to even want to stop at her table. They kept passing her and with each missed opportunity, her desperation grew.

She started making up stories to entice the few potential buyers that stopped. They all seemed more interested in quilts and apple pies. Margaret told one man it was to raise money for her sick grandchild. While she did not have any grandchildren, it turned out that the man had an autistic grandchild of his own. By the time they finished their conversation, she wanted to give him some money, but she had none and knew she could not offer it if she did.

Margaret did not want to admit to herself that she was lying to these people. She needed to make a sale and she justified her embellishments as a necessity.

With the next couple, Margaret changed her story to that of an amateur art historian. She reasoned that if she seemed more knowledgeable, then someone might be more inclined to buy.

"My grandfather painted these," she told the man and woman. Margaret looked over at their daughter. The beautiful brown-haired girl wore a kapp and plain dress, like so many of the Amish here today. It seemed odd to Margaret because the parents did not look Amish at all. A beardless husband and wife with no head covering.

While the couple debated which, if any, painting they would buy, Margaret watched the girl. She guessed her to be no more than five years old. However, the girl stared at the paintings almost with a look of recognition. The depth of her clear eyes showed an understanding that Margaret believed many adults never achieved.

"We'll come back on our way out," the husband said.

Margaret wished she had a dollar for every person that said that this morning. They never came back. Another missed sale and Margaret's spirit sank a little lower.

When she looked to the other end of the table, the little girl was still standing there. Her parents walked off without her. Margaret must not have noticed before, but the girl seemed to be crying. Tears sparkled on her cheeks. She must have been lost already. That couple must not have been her parents, deduced Margaret. The little girl only stopped to look at the paintings by coincidence.

Margaret looked around for somebody, anybody that could help. She knew no one here and could not differentiate any of the show organizers from the customers. She wanted badly to help this little girl. Margaret turned back to give her a comforting word and the girl was gone. She could not leave her table, could not risk losing her paintings to a quick-handed thief when she was not looking. She hoped nothing bad would happen to that little girl.

The girl disappeared so fast that Margaret barely had time to process it. She even considered, after the fact, that she possibly imagined the girl. She had been around the Amish before and there were plenty here today. Maybe, with her exceptional feelings of loss, she projected some of her pain on a make believe child. Maybe, she thought, the child represented her in her own mind. Lost and alone in a chaotic, uncaring world.

Margaret slowly gave up hope after that strange encounter. It seemed her last sacrifice went unnoticed and her prayers to God went unheard.

Ben Abrim, Mr. Kinzinger, and Phil finished their business, while Allan waited with Ruth. He held firmly to her little hand, determined not to let her out of his sight. He even considered sleeping in the kids' room tonight.

Ruth stood on the toe of Allan's boot. Holding onto his hand, she leaned back and swung from side-to-side. Her tears dried swiftly, but her eyes still looked red. The smile on her face told him she was not scared by what happened. Apparently, her imaginary friend Isaac made her feel quite safe.

Allan wanted to discuss the situation more with Ben Abrim. First, he wanted to get home and tell Mary about it all. She had a way of understanding these things. Even leading up to meeting and marrying her ten years ago, Allan felt the Hand of God in his life. He did not necessarily believe in spirits or ghosts walking the earth. At the same time, he gave thanks that God was active in the lives of his children.

Leaving the fair, Ruth pulled Allan toward a corner table as they walked down the wide aisle. The items for sale on this table instantly caught his attention. She had six paintings on display and they looked very familiar to him.

Ben Abrim stopped short and put his hand on Allan's shoulder when he saw them. He pointed at the one that looked most familiar to Allan. Without a doubt, the cabin on the hill had to be Shepherd Tunstile's old place, the house Allan gave to his daughter for her wedding present. It looked almost the same in the painting as when he saw it yesterday. The green of the trees made him think the artist painted it in the early spring. No crops had started up in the fields behind the house.

Occasionally, they had visitors to Karsten Field, outsiders asking to take pictures or walk amongst their simple homes. Some of the older Karsteners did not like the Englishers around their homes. Allan did not mind sharing his blessings. He hoped the outsiders would find some peace on their visit and maybe take that peace back out into the world. If even one person came closer to God, then His glory would shine that much brighter.

Still, Allan could not recall any artists in Karsten Field in recent years. He thought maybe the paintings had been done before he moved there. One thing made him think otherwise. The barn in this lady's painting looked identical to the one he built after his son, Brett, accidentally set fire to the original one. He wondered how someone could spend so much time painting these different scenes of his home and he not notice them.

"Please, tell me, from where did you obtain these artworks?" Ben Abrim asked the woman behind the table.

She looked unsure of her answer. Allan thought she looked sad.

She said, "My grandfather..."

The woman stopped mid-sentence. Allan caught the hint of a tear in her eye. She seemed filled with a great sadness and maybe some guilt. She bit her lip and then her whole body seemed to relax. She apparently made some internal decision that freed her of some pain.

"That's not true," she started. "My husband. I found these in my attic after my husband passed away." She stopped and sighed deeply. "I'm not sure. I think he painted them before we were married."

Ben Abrim pushed up the brim of his hat. Allan looked at his old friend and recognized that crooked smile, slightly different from his normal grin. Ben Abrim knew something about the paintings and he was about to share it.

"I think they are much older than that. I am glad you spoke the truth; I think you will find comfort in honest words. How much are you asking for them?" he said.

The woman looked shocked, as if maybe she had not expected to sell them at all. Ben Abrim's question also surprised Allan. It was not their way to indulge in art or vain possessions. He wondered what Ben Abrim hoped to accomplish.

"I am asking one hundred dollars each, but for you, I could take a little discount if you wanted to buy them all. I guess five hundred," she said.

Ben Abrim turned to Allan. He asked, "Mr. Howarth, how much do we have left in that bundle."

Allan did not have to count it. He had been entrusted to protect their finances on this trip and he paid close attention, with one exception. When he thought Ruth was missing, he left the money unattended. He knew it had no value if he lost his child. After they concluded their business, Allan counted the remaining money and stuffed it deep in his pocket.

He whispered, as not to share their business with nearby Englishers, "It is eight hundred."

"That is good," said Ben Abrim. He turned back to the woman and said, "I will give you eight hundred U.S. dollars for all six paintings with one condition; you must deliver them personally to Mr. Kinzinger's restaurant in Karsten Field. Do you know the place? It is down the interstate some few miles."

The woman apparently could not help it any longer. She cried openly. Ben Abrim obviously gave her some blessing that she never expected. Allan knew the value of money to the outside world. After their recent troubles, he thanked God for their boon. It seemed right that they should share it with others, strangers even, that needed it more than they did.

Phil took over the conversation and gave the lady directions. Allan handed the money to Mr. Kinzinger and he stepped out of the way with Ruth.

"I liked those pictures," said Ruth. "Isaac says his friend painted them."

When Ben Abrim came close, Allan asked him, "Do you know what this child speaks?"

He nodded. "I do. And I should tell you, I never thought I would see one of those paintings."

"Are you going to tell me? That barn looks like Alice and Samuel's barn," said Allan.

"Do you think the one that burned was the original?" said Ben Abrim. "Mr. Tunstile built his barn to accommodate that troublesome generator. There was one that stood before. The one in that painting that looks so much like yours."

Allan shifted Ruth's grasp from one hand to the other. The mystery of these paintings peaked his curiosity. He said, "These paintings are quite old then?"

Ben Abrim turned his grin on Allan. He said, "If you want to hear the story, some of which you know, join me when our new friend Margaret comes to deliver them."

Margaret could not believe her sudden fortune. Not only did she sell all six paintings, but also that peculiar little Amish man paid more than she asked. As she drove toward their town, she felt her spirit lifted for the first time in weeks. She thought of her Stephen sitting next to her, instead of the paintings occupying the front seat of her car. The man named Ben Abrim promised her a story about the paintings. She thought that maybe he knew where they came from and who painted them.

At this point, Margaret hoped it would be revealed that Stephen came to Karsten Field once and was inspired to paint. As she steered her car into a diagonal parking spot in front of Kinzinger's Restaurant, she started to doubt that feeling which had been so strong since coming down from her attic.

She knew Ben Abrim would be waiting for her inside the restaurant. She hoped that the little girl would be there too. She did not get a chance to ask her name or anything about her. Obviously, she was with her father, holding his hand. Somehow, she must have led the men back to her.

At the time, she thought the girl was lost and wanted desperately to help her. In the end, it seemed, the little girl helped her instead. She must have liked the paintings and brought her father and his friends back to the table.

Inside, Ben Abrim waited with warm apple pie. Margaret could not resist the offer. She had a weakness for sweets that Stephen rarely would indulge. While she ate, Ben Abrim introduced everyone in the restaurant. Mr. Howarth brought his wife, Mary, and their two children Benjamin and Ruth. Margaret wanted to hold Ruth and squeeze her.

She said to Ruth, "I think you are my guardian angel. I don't have any grandchildren of my own, but if I did, I would want them to be exactly like you."

Ruth giggled and said, "I'm not an angel. My friend Isaac is and he says God has enough angels to protect all of his children."

After everyone finished his or her pie, Ben Abrim started his story. "These paintings go back to the beginnings of Karsten Field, to a young man named Simon Lengacher."

Without another word, Margaret knew what that *S* in the lower right hand corner of each painting meant. A man named Simon painted these, not her husband Stephen. It did not explain why Stephen had them in their attic though.

Ben Abrim continued, "Simon left Karsten Field to pursue a talent which he believed God gave him. I know that the Lord speaks to us all in different ways and cannot say the young Mr.

Lengacher left the faith for no good cause. I heard that he believed sacrificing his salvation might help others find theirs through his artworks. I believe a friend told him that his efforts would only ensure his salvation too. Sacrificing yourself before God is the ultimate sign of trust. God does not ask for this sacrifice, but raises up those that put Him before all else."

The talk of sacrifice stunned Margaret. Those ideas occupied her mind these past several days. She felt like she was giving up everything; her home, her possessions, her last connection to the man she loved. In a flash, she understood everything. Before Stephen died, her relationship with God had not been strong. Because of that, she had no one to lean on when she lost her husband. She did not know God well enough to find comfort with Him. Like this story of Simon Lengacher or Abraham and Isaac from the bible, God asked for her sacrifice to know where she placed Him in her life. It literally took losing everything to find what she was missing.

Now, for the first time since Stephen got sick, Margaret felt peace. When she woke up this morning to deliver the paintings, her heart did not hurt. Sacrificing that last physical connection with her husband let God know how she felt and what she believed. Without realizing what she was doing, she showed her trust in God by giving up everything. Already, He was bestowing her with blessings. First, Ben Abrim gave her more money than she needed and now she felt a welcoming comfort with the people of Karsten Field.

They spent the rest of the day touring Karsten and looking at the buildings from the paintings. For the paintings being around one hundred years old, everything looked amazingly the same. There were more houses by the Fencil place and Alice's barn looked newer.

Nearing sunset, Ben Abrim lead Margaret to the field where Simon depicted his friend being lifted up by an angel. The way the sun beamed over the treetops, made the golden wheat glow like it did in the painting. The little girl, Ruth, held her hand.

This made Margaret weep. However, she did not cry in pain. She felt God's joy in her heart and it was unbelievable. She did not know how many more years she would have in this life, but she knew she would not spend them alone.

CHAPTER FIVE

AWAY IN A MANGER

Ruth always looked forward to the end of harvest. For her five-year-old mind, it meant Christmas was next. It did not matter to her that it was the end of October. She did not keep track of time the same way adults do. The hard work of the summer was over and soon the snow would come.

Alice and Samuel started a tradition after the twins were born. Samuel kept a pumpkin patch down the backside of their house. He cut three rows out of the way of his main fields so the cows would not trample the orange orbs. Having the pumpkins meant the other Karsteners would not have to wait for the fair to get their jars of pumpkin, and that meant fresher pumpkin pie.

Ruth did not particularly like pumpkin pie. She liked the day they went out to pick the last pumpkin. Samuel always saved one big pumpkin for Ruth, her brother and her niece and nephew. The kids made their way through a tangle of drying vines. The vines no longer had to be green since they had only one pumpkin to deliver water and nutrients. This year, big brother Benjamin used his father's hatchet to cut the prize from the hardened vine. Apparently, their Datt thought he was old enough to handle such a task.

Once loose, Isaac, Elizabeth and Ruth crowded around the huge treasure. They worked in unison to lift and carry the pumpkin toward the house. Much to the delight of their watching parents, this did not go smoothly. The three younger children could not manage to walk in the same direction at the same time. They stumbled through the twisted vines and dropped the pumpkin more than once. Before they completed the journey, Ruth, Isaac and Elizabeth resorted to rolling it with Benjamin directing them from behind as if he was driving a team of mules. Somehow, the pumpkin never cracked or burst.

"Giddyap," Benjamin shouted, eliciting a roar of laughter from his father.

Eventually, they made it to the front steps where Samuel took over the job. His strong arms wrapped easily around the pumpkin that the three of them could not lift. Then it disappeared into the cabin. Ruth did not follow like the other kids. She did not wait to watch it sliced open. She did not take pleasure in Alice scooping the stringy mess out of it. Surely, they would have pumpkin pie after their family dinner, but Ruth would not eat it. Instead, she walked back over to the patch. Her mother, Mary, usually walked with her. They stared at the bare vines that brought their friends and family so much joy.

Ruth liked what the empty pumpkin patch meant. It meant Christmas.

Two months may pass quickly for an adult. For a parent, it happens even faster. Ruth, however, counted the days almost as years. She tried to help her Mamm around the house. She tried to stay busy. Being too young for school, she did not have studies to occupy her time and she had to wait for her brother or anybody to play. The time ticked slowly along its own path.

Ruth wondered about time. She wondered where it came from and where it went. Who decided what time it was and why was it so important? It did not matter to her what hour or day it was. Except Saturdays and Sundays. Those were important to her because her whole family could be together the whole day. Other than that, time passed like the river where she sometimes watched her father go fishing. A day might pass like a leaf floating on the river. Sometimes, it would shoot right by with barely enough time to look at it. Other times, it would get caught in a swirl and hang around until she thought it might wash ashore and stick in the mud. Either way, Ruth had no idea where the leaf came from or where it went.

Her days passed like that, some fast, some slow, until the first snow of winter. That first snow day, aside from its biting cold, felt almost as good as the last pumpkin day. Her Mamm would bundle her tight and Ruth would head out into a transformed world. Her boots would crunch the covered ground under her weight. It felt funny to her to have boots on compared to the barefoot summer. They had a transition period where her Mamm would tell her to put shoes on when she went outside. Ruth avoided that as much as possible, until it got cold enough to curl her toes.

With low, gray clouds and a solid white ground, the world seemed strangely quiet. Ruth could hear squirrels chittering half way to Alice's house. She guessed they had not gathered enough nuts and now they scrambled through the snow in hopes of finding a few more. Her Datt always told her work first and then there would be time to play.

This was her time to play.

She would find somewhere out of sight of Benjamin and his snowballs. She would look for a low hanging branch decorated with icicles and snap one off for herself. The cold, melting water felt good on her lips. Ruth would sit and listen to Isaac Karsten, her guardian angel, tell her all about the first Christmas as she licked her frozen treat.

That first snow did not usually last long. Sometimes, they had snow for Christmas. Sometimes, they did not. It did not start to get really cold until January and that is when their outside playtime ended until the warmer weather returned.

About a week before Christmas, Mamm dismissed school for the winter break. Then Ruth would have both of her parents. She could help her Mamm with kitchen chores or go exploring the woods with her Datt. If they had a lot of snow, he would take her across the frozen river and go deep into the woods. They would find a place to sit together and watch for deer.

Anytime Allan asked, "Are you cold?"

"No," Ruth would answer. She did not want to tell him yes, no matter how red her nose got. Days like this, she wanted them to swirl on for hours and hours, like that lonely leaf stuck in a current.

One morning, Mr. Kinzinger came to their house for a visit. He looked excited as he said, "I have received the most wonderful news."

"What could that be?" asked Mary. She plopped her ball of dough on the counter and turned to face Allan and Mr. Kinzinger. She had flour smeared on both cheeks and this made Ruth laugh. Mary shook her hands at her daughter and loose flour drifted down like an indoor snowstorm. Ruth giggled more and almost missed Mr. Kinzinger's news.

"Our friend, Mr. William Bowman has called and asked if his family can join us for a Christmas Dinner," said Mr. Kinzinger.

"Surely you said *yes*," said Allan, patting Mr. Kinzinger on the back.

Ruth liked the idea of seeing the Bowman's again. It seemed so long since that hot summer day when they came to visit. Mr. Bowman's son, Chris, was very nice to her. Ruth thought of Christmas as a time for sharing, so it could only be better to share it with more people.

"Does that mean Miss Margaret will be here too?" asked Ruth.

Miss Margaret had visited almost every Saturday since Ben Abrim bought those special paintings from her. Ruth sincerely hoped all of her friends could be together.

"That is a wonderful idea, mein herz," answered Mary. Ruth liked that her Mamm always said she had good ideas, even if they did not follow them.

As usual, the first snow melted away leaving a muddy mess in some of Ruth's favorite play areas. With only a few days until their friends arrived for the Christmas dinner, the weather did not disappoint Ruth. A light snow started early in the morning before she awoke. Once the sun came up, Ruth sat in her bed watching the ground slowly turn from brown to white. The little flakes did not look very threatening, but they did not stop either.

There had been a lot of discussion among the adults about inviting so many outsiders for one of the most important days in Karsten Field. Ruth did not think she was supposed to hear Ben Abrim talking to Mr. Fencil. However, she was in the room, so as far as she was concerned, she was part of the conversation. At least once a week, Ruth visited Ben Abrim. He usually read to her from the bible and they got around to talking about her guardian angel, Isaac. More than anybody else, he seemed to believe her the most.

During this visit, Matthew Fencil came to talk about the Christmas dinner. He said that some of the families did not feel it was right to have outsiders celebrating the birth of their Lord with them. It was not their way to mingle so easily with the Englishers.

"Who feels thusly?" asked Ben Abrim. Ruth liked when he used his fancy words. That meant he was serious.

Mr. Fencil said, "My mother and the rest of our family. The Millers do not plan to attend, nor any of the Ottos. I have yet to speak on it with Mr. Esch or Mr. Troyer."

Ben Abrim smiled. He always smiled, recalled Ruth. He said, "It appears as many in Karsten Field are closed to it as those that are open to it. I propose an amenable solution. Mr. Kinzinger is inclined to open his restaurant for the occasion. Those that will meet with our English friends will find a seat at his table. We can celebrate with them the day before and we will have three days of Christmas this year."

"You plan to have a Christmas Eve dinner then?" asked Mr. Fencil.

"Only if we will not be shunned for it," said Ben Abrim. Ruth thought he might be joking about that. She did not completely understand what shunning meant, but she did not think it was good.

Mr. Fencil stood from the seat at Ben Abrim's reading table. He put on his hat and moved toward the front door. He said, "I will allow certain indulgences to a man of your age. Keep in the front of your mind the reason for this day."

"I know the meaning of Christmas as well as this child here," said Ben Abrim. He patted Ruth on the head. She had not expected to be brought into the conversation. Mr. Fencil did not often take time to acknowledge children when he had such important things to discuss. Ben Abrim continued, "It is a time to open our hearts. Our savior was born in a stable because no one would make room for Mary and Joseph. Maybe we should think to make room for those that do not seem to belong. Our English friends brought many blessings to Karsten Field. What better time to show them our thanks? The good Lord brought them into our lives that we may continue to live and serve Him according to our ways."

Mr. Fencil had nothing else to say and left Ben Abrim and Ruth alone. Ben Abrim's smile faded for a moment, so Ruth gave him one of her own. She found that her smiles made other people smile even when they looked sad. It worked with Ben Abrim and they went back to their reading.

The last place Ruth wanted to be on the day of their Christmas meal was her mother's kitchen. She was not quite old enough to help with the whirlwind of tasks that needed to be accomplished. Her Datt and brother Benjamin made trips back and forth to Mr. Kinzinger's restaurant. Ruth had nothing more to do than watch her Mamm. She did not have the size, speed or knowledge to keep up with her mother. Ruth wondered if everybody's house in the whole world went crazy for Christmas.

When things finally settled, it came time for her whole family to go to the restaurant. Ruth walked behind her mother, carrying a jar of preserves she could not identify. Datt and Benjamin led the way, both with one last armful of food. The light snow that started two days ago had not stopped. It did not come down any stronger, only slow and steady. Ruth left deep prints in the accumulating snow and the hem of her dress only partially brushed them away.

The snow covered everything on the main street. Ruth could not tell where the sidewalk turned into road, except where Eli Gundy shoveled big clumps from the parking spaces in front of the restaurant. They had no need for them, but Ruth knew the Bowmans and Miss Margaret would have to put their cars somewhere. She did not see any buggies, so she could not tell who was already inside the restaurant. It made Ruth happy that no one would make their horses stand outside in this cold while they ate dinner.

Ben Abrim waited for them while they came inside and stomped the snow off their boots before walking across the vitrified floor tiles. The Kurtz family was already there too and Ethel was trying to get somebody to start singing with her.

The Bowmans arrived next. Ruth watched out the foggy window as their car rolled to a stop in one of the two spaces cleared by Eli Gundy. Even in the short time since he came inside to warm up, the black asphalt had turned white again.

"My goodness, those roads are getting bad out there," exclaimed Mr. Bowman as he unwrapped his scarf. He stopped to help his wife take off her long black coat. Underneath she wore a dress that both excited and worried Ruth. The almost maroon material sparkled like no clothes Ruth had ever seen. None of Ruth's dresses ever sparkled. She worried for Mrs. Bowman though, because the dress looked too short. It did not cover anything below her knees or on her shoulders. Ruth wondered how Mrs. Bowman could stand to be outside at all.

Her Mamm was helping Mrs. Kinzinger and the other mothers in the kitchen, so Ruth had no one to ask about the beautiful and frightening dress. She decided on her own that it was not something she would wear. She felt tempted by its looks and that gave her a funny feeling. Suddenly, Mrs. Gundy appeared from the kitchen, wrapped a shawl around Mrs. Bowman's bare shoulders and disappeared, with only a whisper in Mrs. Bowman's ear. Ruth thought she understood something about modesty and left it at that.

Young Chris Bowman came and sat next to Ruth in her window booth. He said *hi*. She said *hi* and then they sat quietly. Benjamin climbed into the booth with them and stared at Chris. The Bowmans had not been back to Karsten Field since the hot, hot summer. Not only were they outsiders, but they were also African-American Englishers. Apparently, Chris's darker skin color held a fascination for Benjamin.

Eventually, places were set and the children instructed to wash their hands. Dinner would be served at six o'clock, as planned. Since five-thirty, Ben Abrim took to standing at the door. He watched the slow steady flakes cover the Bowmans' car. The parking spot cleared for Margaret was no longer distinguishable from the rest of the street.

Ruth heard her Datt ask Ben Abrim what he was doing.

"It is not like Miss Margaret to be late. I pray nothing has happened to her, travelling in this weather," said Ben Abrim.

When it came time to put food on the table, Margaret had not yet arrived. Ben Abrim looked truly worried. Ruth wanted to help watch, so she knelt in her booth with her nose against the cold glass window. The low clouds blocked the moon, so she could only see about as far as the lights stretched out into the street. She saw a rectangular patch of snow that held one car hostage.

Everyone sat quietly, waiting for Ben Abrim to take his seat. Silent prayers were said for Miss Margaret's safety.

Ruth's sister Alice said, "Maybe she decided not to go out in the storm."

"Why would she not call?" asked Mr. Kinzinger. "She has the telephone number for the one there on the wall," he said, pointing at the payphone. Apparently to underline his point, he scooted his chair back and went to the phone. He picked it up and listened for a moment. Ruth thought he made a strange face and then hung up the phone.

"Very strange. There is no line," said Mr. Kinzinger.

"What do you mean?" asked Ben Abrim.

"We have no dial tone. The storm must have stopped the service. Even if Miss Margaret wanted to call, we would not receive it," explained Mr. Kinzinger.

Ben Abrim seemed most troubled of all by this news. Sharing the connection of the paintings now hanging on the walls of Mr. Kinzinger's restaurant created a strong friendship between the two of them. Ruth had seen one of the Troyer boys courting Katie Menlach. She did not think Ben Abrim would be acting so silly, but the thought made her smile. Miss Margaret would have to be baptized first though, Ruth knew.

The moment before Ben Abrim took his seat, Ruth shouted, "I see something!"

Outside, in the dark, at the far end of the street, Ruth spotted a pair of approaching lights. She had seen enough cars in her short life to know what headlights look like. Ben Abrim almost knocked his chair over coming back to the door. Her Datt and Mr. Kinzinger followed. In a moment, half the people gathered for dinner stood out on the sidewalk while the rest crowded around the window. Ruth felt squished between her brother and her cousin Elizabeth.

Aside from the feeling of being smushed, Ruth felt something else. She felt a sense of belonging. Every person here, everyone in Karsten Field, cared so much about everybody else. They loved outsiders even as they would their own family. To Ruth, Karsten Field was more than a church district, it was home and it was family. All of them showed concern for Miss Margaret while their food started to cool on the table. It was more important to all of them that even one of them was safe than it was to be on time for dinner. Ruth felt crushed, but she also felt love.

Laughter and cheers erupted when Miss Margaret stopped her car in front of Mr. Kinzinger's restaurant. Miss Margaret climbed out of her car. The driver's door creaked on its old hinges loud enough that Ruth could hear it on her side of the glass. Ben Abrim and her Datt helped Margaret from the car. The commotion stopped when the back door of Miss Margaret's car opened.

A young man emerged, wearing only a thin jacket and no hat. He had a short haircut, almost to being bald, and his beard circled only his mouth, covering his upper lip. It did not grow up the sides of his face. He had darker skin, but not quite as dark as Mr. Bowman. The man looked around at all of the people watching him. Then he turned back to the car. He helped a young woman from her seat. She looked like she needed the extra help. Despite being skinny, she had a huge belly. Ruth guessed it had to be full with a baby.

This woman, too, had dark skin. She looked darker than the man, still, Ruth understood that they were not the same as African-Americans. She had long black hair that hung down in shiny curls past her shoulders. She did not cover her head either. Ruth noticed shiny metal hanging from the woman's ears and shades of blue and purple painted across her eyelids. This woman wore make-up like Miss Margaret, but not nearly as much as Mrs. Bowman.

The young couple looked scared. Neither of them dressed warm enough for the cold and the woman kept rubbing her hands across her belly. The man reached back in the car and pulled out a suitcase. The handle, once broken, had been repaired with wide, silver tape. It had scratches along the bottom like it had been used a lot.

"Why are we standing out here? Let's get inside," said Allan. Ruth liked when her Datt took charge. She always thought of him as a strong man.

Everybody followed Allan's suggestion and filed back through the restaurant door. The women wasted no time setting two new places for the quiet, soon-to-be parents. Ruth watched the pregnant woman closely and got a timid smile in response. Neither of Miss Margaret's guests said a word.

Ben Abrim stood to offer a prayer. He said, "Before we are introduced to our new guests, I think we should bless this meal and give thanks for everyone gathered here this evening. Once we get the spoons and forks to moving, I think there will be plenty of time to meet our new friends. They look as hungry as I feel."

Then Ben Abrim lowered his head and gave thanks to God in celebration of the birth of His son.

As utensils clinked against plates and laughter darted across the room, Ruth listened close to Ben Abrim talking to Miss Margaret. He said, "Please tell me who you have brought with you tonight. I assume that is what caused you to be so late."

Miss Margaret swallowed a bite of mashed potatoes. After wiping her mouth, she said, "These are my new friends, Jose and Maria. Thank you for being so hospitable. I don't think they have anywhere else to go."

At the mention of their names, Ruth noticed both the man and woman lowered their heads. Even after this much time, neither of them said a word. Ruth asked, "Can they talk?"

Margaret smiled and said, "They can, but I think they speak mostly Spanish. Do you speak Spanish, my dear?"

Ruth answered, "I speak only English like my Datt. I don't even speak them funny words like Mamm when she tells me to do my chores. She hasn't taught it to me yet. Can you speak Spanish, Miss Margaret?"

"I took a class a few years ago, before my Stephen got sick. Mostly, it was something to do while he was at work. I remember enough, I think. The best that I can understand, Jose lost his job in Chicago. They were heading to Kansas City, I think. If I understood him, they have family there. I was driving on the highway to come visit you when I saw their flashing lights. Something happened to their car. I thought maybe they were out of gas, so we tried to find a gas station open this late on Christmas Eve. Maria was going to wait with their car, but I wouldn't have it. There was no way I was going to leave this precious, pregnant young girl out to freeze. I hope you don't mind that I brought them here."

Ben Abrim put a hand on Margaret's shoulder. He looked on the verge of tears, but still held that familiar smile. With his free hand, he pushed his empty plate toward the middle of the table. He said, "If I have learned one thing from my dear friend Allan, it is that you never know who God puts in your path or for what reason. We do not have many friends from the outside, but those we do have are special indeed. You have all come to us through unique circumstances, guided by God's unseen hand. Jose and Maria are no exception. They needed someplace safe and warm tonight and our provident Lord sent you, Miss Margaret, to deliver them to our door. Of course they are welcome."

Jose smiled again. He seemed very shy. Ruth heard him whisper a word that sounded like *grassy* and the name for a donkey that her Mamm did not allow her to say. Ruth imagined a grassy-donkey would be quite a funny sight.

Maybe, she guessed, in Spanish it meant *thank you*.

Once the empty plates had been cleared away, Ben Abrim led another prayer. Ruth noticed they ate most of the food. She thought with the amount they made, that it would take a week to eat it all. What was left would not be enough for her and Benjamin's lunch the next day. She knew an assortment of pies would be waiting for them; Shoofly, Pumpkin, Apple Crumble. First, all of the younger children gathered in the middle of the room and the adults circled around them. The Christmas hymns were some of Ruth's favorites. Maybe she did not sing every church day, but she knew all of the words to the Christmas hymns.

Between songs, the gathered friends and family of Karsten Field took turns sharing stories from Christmas past. They talked of wonderful meals, handmade gifts, blizzards and how much they thanked God for each and every year that they could gather to share in His joy.

During the bustling activity, no one noticed Jose and Maria slip out the front door. The bell barely made a sound over the loud, thankful voices. Ruth caught a fading glimpse of the young couple wandering down the sidewalk, into the dark night. Jose had one arm around Maria and carried their battered suitcase with the other. She tried to interrupt the song, but everyone was having too much fun to notice a five-year-old girl.

When the singing finally ended, Margaret noticed the absence of her friends first out of the adults. She asked with some bewilderment, "Where are Jose and Maria?"

"They left," said Ruth as simply as she could.

Allan came to his daughter and sat on the edge of her booth bench. He asked, "When did they leave, mein herz? Did you see which way they went?"

Ruth pointed out the window past the two snow-covered cars. She said, "They went that way a while ago, maybe like two hours." She had no real idea how long it was, but she wanted to give as much information as she could.

Her Datt, Ben Abrim and several other men went outside, looking for the Hispanic couple. The flurry of snow had only worsened since they started dinner. The men did not stay outside for very long. While Ruth waited on her bench, she heard a few words from her guardian angel, Isaac.

Ben Abrim came inside first. Rubbing his red hands, he said, "The snow has erased their tracks. We cannot tell which way they went. Mr. Howarth thinks maybe they went toward the highway to hitch onto a ride, or something like that."

Ruth said, "Isaac told me not to worry. They are safe."

Ben Abrim gave her one of his confirming smiles. He agreed not to worry, but she knew he would. He was a good man and cared equally for everybody that God delivered into his life. There would be no way for Ben Abrim to search for the couple, but Ruth would help him if she could.

Christmas morning arrived and brought bright sunshine with it.

Samuel Menlach did not rise quite as early as usual, but he still had a few chores to tend to before celebrating the rest of the Lord 's Day with his family and friends. He left his wife, Alice, asleep and peeked in on the twins. They stayed up later than their normal bedtime last night. Samuel and Alice waited with Allan and Mary until everyone else had gone. Mr. Kinzinger locked his restaurant as the Bowman's and Miss Margaret carefully drove away. Samuel herded the twins, while Alice made sure Ben Abrim made it home.

The walk to their cabin did not take too long and at least the snow had stopped falling. As they went inside, Samuel thought he noticed a light in the barn, seeping out under the wide double doors. That made no sense and when he looked a second time, he saw nothing. He decided it was too cold and too late to worry more about it.

The thought of the mystery night light came back to him this morning as he headed down the front steps. The powdery snow crunched beneath his feet all the way to the barn. Why would he imagine something like that, Samuel wondered. It was not like Mr. Kinzinger who often forgot and left his restaurant lights on when he had long gone home to bed. They had no electricity in the barn and Old Mr. Tunstile's generator had long been removed. Even if Samuel wanted a light in the barn, which he reminded himself he did not, there was no way to get the power for it out this far. More than any other Karsteners, they lived without the tempting luxuries of the outside world. Mr. Tunstile may have been less Amish and more friendly with the English, but Samuel would not guess that from the plainness of the old cabin. Once the barn burned a few years back, they all worked together to rebuild it in their traditional fashion.

With all those thoughts running through his head, Samuel became most curious as to what caused that sudden flash of light. He started pulling on the barn door. About eight inches of snow piled up against it and he did not take the time to shovel it clear. By the time he worked it open wide enough to pass through, Samuel started sweating, despite the cold morning.

Inside the barn, he watched the steam from his breath for a moment. He felt a little warmer inside, but not much. The animals with their thick coats did not seem to mind the cold. At least they were out of the wind. If his daughter Elizabeth had her way, the cows would be sleeping in their front room and the chickens would roost in the kitchen cabinets.

Then Samuel heard a noise that he did not quite recognize. He first thought it was the bleating of a lamb, but they did not keep any in their barn. The soft sound came from one of the empty stalls at the far end of the barn. The sound came again. It seemed to touch him in his heart. This time, it sounded more familiar. Samuel thought it was the sound of a cooing baby. He had not heard that sound in at least five years, with Ruth being the youngest member of Karsten Field.

Samuel quietly walked the length of the barn. He carefully peeked around the edge of the stall. He did not want to surprise anybody that might be hiding there. That kind of shock could lead to an altercation and he did not want that. To his delight, a baby boy lay in the straw, his body wrapped in one of Mr. Kinzinger's hand-stitched tablecloths. The baby laughed when he made eye contact with Samuel. On either side, in the mound of hay, the baby's exhausted parents, Jose and Maria, slept soundly. At their feet, he saw the opened suitcase, which contained a flashlight among the clothes and other necessities.

The mystery of the secret late night light had been solved. Now, Samuel had to decide what to do about the people in his barn.

Making his way silently out of the barn, Samuel sent his son to spread the word to Allan, Ben Abrim and the others. Alice prepared a breakfast for their unexpected guests while they waited for the others to arrive. It did not take long for Eli Gundy to harness his horses and deliver a sled full of folks to Samuel's barn. By then, Jose and Maria awoke and looked completely embarrassed. Between the two of them, they did not possess enough English to express themselves. Samuel heard them repeatedly say *gracias* and *lo siento*. He had no idea what the words meant, but their gestures and expressions made him think they were either saying *thank you* or *sorry*.

Ruth watched the whole scene with fascination.

Jose and Maria ate their breakfast while Mary and Alice tended to the baby. They wrapped the boy child in proper blankets after washing him with some warm towels. They were careful not to take the child too far from his mother since they had no way to communicate their intentions. Mary told Allan she would like to give the child a proper bath, but neither of them knew if Maria would allow it.

When the baby was dry, Mary helped his mother to feed him. The new mother looked to have no experience with this. Benjamin yelled "Ick" and ran out of the barn. Ruth had a vague memory of her Mamm sharing milk with her in this way and wanted to watch. She thought it was amazing how a mother could share a part of herself with her baby.

Finally, Ben Abrim arrived with Mr. Kinzinger. Ruth listened as they talked with her Datt.

Mr. Kinzinger said, "I spoke with Margaret and she is coming soon. She tells me there is a shelter in Des Moines that will house them for a few days. We should all pray that the charitable people there are able to contact this young couple's family down in Missouri."

The new baby cooed and giggled now that it had a full belly and a warm blanket. The parents seemed much happier, much less scared than they did the night before. Ruth believed her imaginary friend Isaac when he told her they would be safe. She never expected to find them in this barn. It reminded her of the story of another baby whose parents had nowhere else to go. No one would give them a place to sleep, so that baby was born in a manger. Ben Abrim told Ruth that a manger was a lot like a barn when he read that story to her.

That connection made Ruth ask a question. She said, "Is this the baby Jesus?"

Ben Abrim laughed and a few of the other adults smiled. The outsider Jose looked at Ruth. He repeated, "Jesus," but it sounded more like *Heysus*. Ruth thought this Spanish language sounded funny.

Jose repeated *Heysus* to Maria. He said a few other words that Ruth did not understand. Then Maria responded, "Si, bueno. Me gusta el nombre de Jesus."

Ruth's Mamm hugged her daughter and explained, "This is not our savior Jesus Christ, but it looks like our new friends like the name for their baby."

Ruth looked around the barn as other families from Karsten Field came into Samuel and Alice's barn. They all came to see the new baby, even Matthew Fencil and his family. Everyone was there to celebrate new life. Ruth understood that it did not matter whether they were Amish, English or Hispanic. She liked that about Christmas. It was a time of sharing and compassion, a time when people showed how much they loved each other. Ruth wished every Christmas could be this special. Then, for a five year old, she made an incredible revelation. As long as she was with her friends and family and could share her heart, every Christmas would be the greatest.

CHAPTER SIX

TOUCHED BY FIRE

Brett almost did not recognize himself sitting on that pile of straw. He looked down at himself like he was watching a movie. This version of Brett had to be around fourteen or fifteen years old and he still had a lot to learn.

Older Brett, wiser Brett, tried to understand what he was seeing. The younger boy leaned back in a pile of hay and hay covered the dimly lit ground, scattered around him. Shadows closed in on all sides, making it impossible to see much further than the pile. The only light seemed to come from something in the boy's hands. The rectangular object threw a bluish-purple glow onto the boy's smooth face, so different to the wrinkles that already started to show around older Brett's eyes.

A game. It is a game, Brett realized. His younger self is playing a hand-held video game, he told himself. Strange, he thought, that the device did not look like any unit he knew of. He should know every system out there. That was his job now. Whatever was happening, things did not seem to be exactly right in this world. Why would he be alone in a pile of straw, playing a game he never played?

The boy continued playing the game, unaware of his older observer hovering somewhere above him. Brett wanted to call out to the younger version of himself, but he did not know what to say.

Should he offer some advice for the future? Should he ask for help from a younger, innocent perspective? There had been plenty of movies and books on the subject of meeting or trading places with your younger self. Some suggested to never interfere, while others showed a lesson to be learned from the encounter.

Brett wondered what lesson he might learn from watching himself play a video game in a barn.

A barn.

Suddenly, Brett realized when and where this was. He remembered the event clearly. It changed his life and it was the part of Karsten Field that he always carried with him in his heart.

Brett knew what to expect next and he dreaded it. As if on cue, the hand-held video game emitted a beep. The screen started flashing red. The alternating lights from red to that bluish color made the boy's face look strange, maybe a little scared.

In a place without electricity, there would be only one possible way to charge the device's batteries.

The generator.

The previous owner of the barn had not always followed the strict Amish ways. The man, long gone from this world, kept a gas-powered generator in the barn. Sometime or another, he had use for electricity. His neighbors might have called it a weakness. In any case, it had not been used in years, even before the old man went to walk with God.

Then, there came a time when young Brett felt like he deserved to use it. He felt like he earned it. Unbeknownst to his parents, he snuck out to the barn to gain his reward. Now, he wandered out into the dark with only a flashing red light to guide him. Brett did not remember the barn being so big as it now appeared. It seemed almost cavernous. Young Brett continued to walk forward while old Brett watched with growing trepidation.

Eventually, the boy came to a wall, a dirty metal wall. But it was not exactly a wall. Covered in dials, knobs and levers, the dull rusty metal stretched high out of sight. It extended in either direction, swallowed by blackness. It might as well have been a wall, but it was not. It was the generator.

Brett remembered it being only as tall as himself. This twisted version of the generator loomed over the desperate boy. It taunted him with a single outlet right at the center of his reach.

Nothing seemed right to older Brett. In fact, it all seemed far worse, an exaggerated account of a haunting memory. Brett worried about what came next. On lonely nights when sleep could not find him, he often wished to change what came next. At this moment, he wanted to shout at the boy.

"Don't touch it." He felt like he screamed, but he could not even hear his own voice. He knew the boy could not possibly hear him.

Young Brett uncoiled a wire from his pocket. One end, he easily connected to the video game unit in his hand. The other end dangled for a moment like the end of a pendulum counting time into an unknown infinity.

As the teenager lifted the dual pronged wire toward the receptacle, Older Brett watched sparks dance between the closing distance. Blue streaks popped and cracked. They became more frequent and more intense as the metal plug neared the outlet. The young boy did not seem to notice the electric display that should have warned him of the danger. Instead, he jammed the plug into the slot.

Nothing happened.

Older Brett expected at least a burst of energy, if not an explosion. Why no show? Of course, the generator needed to be running. Younger Brett needed to push the big red button. That young boy knew very little of mechanics. He did not know to check for gas or oil. He only knew to push the button. The bright red circle did not give him cause to hesitate. It should have been a warning. In nature, God gave things a red color to keep others away. The red color of this button should have done the same thing, but it did not deter that determined boy.

The button clicked under the pressure of young Brett's thumb. A moment later, internal valves hesitantly opened to allow fuel through its dusty lines, pouring directly toward a spark generated by that button click.

Ignition.

The monstrous generator roared to life, because big scary things always roar when they come to life. It moaned and grumbled. Dials spun and gears creaked. Older Brett could see jumping straw on the floor, a result of vibrations from the massive machine.

Electricity had to be flowing to the game unit now, but the light still flashed red. Young Brett randomly flipped levers and pushed more buttons on the generator. He looked desperate. After a frantic attack on the generator, he looked at the game again. The light stopped flashing, went dark and then suddenly illuminated a solid orange. Someone, at some point, chose orange as the universal color to indicate charging. The orange glow brought a smile to young Brett's face.

The charge lasted less than a minute. Not enough juice to even turn on the game. Then the generator coughed black smoke from the vents along the floor. The smoke rose and quickly faded into the shadows. A moment later, it coughed again and then belched fire. Small licks of flame rolled out across the floor, grabbing for any straw they could get. The single reeds spun wildly, reaching for their friends, hoping to be saved. Instead of salvation, the burning hay spread the fire to more hay, circling young Brett before he could react. In an instant, raging flames beat the shadows back to the walls of the barn and the fire feasted on the dry, old timbers.

Older, wiser Brett snapped awake from his nightmare. He wiped sweat from his forehead on his thousand-thread count bed sheet. He thought the warmth from his dream carried over into his waking morning, then realized that Kat had cranked the furnace again. She never seemed too concerned that his computers needed to be kept cool.

Brett dropped his bare feet to the dark, polished wood floor and stared at the white wall above his dresser. It took a moment for him to fully remember his dream. When he did, he knew it was the same dream he had countless times over the years. The memory of the barn fire stayed with him and always resurfaced during stressful times in his life. He knew he was responsible for setting fire to his father's barn, but the dream always made it seem so much worse. During his college finals, the nightmare struck with such force that Brett almost did not sleep. Even bleary eyed, he still pulled out a ninety percent on his Linear Algebra test.

Maybe he had not paid attention to the dreams before that. He recalled having them in high school and occasionally at the beginning of his college career. After college graduation, significant events triggered the shadows and flames in his sleep more regularly. When he started his software company, they kept him awake. When his game *Barn Burners* sold enough copies to go *gold*, they kept him awake. Lately, when Kat started making demands on their relationship, they returned.

Katherina Verona, or Kat as she preferred, currently occupied the kitchen, from the smell of brewing coffee. They became exclusive almost eight months ago. Finally, this past week, she spent the night at his apartment for the first time. By the end of the week, she stayed over three nights, she cranked the furnace three mornings and he had the generator nightmare three times.

He loved Kat. Brett knew that in his heart. They shared everything and their relationship grew. She managed the publicity for his video game company and orchestrated a promotional tour for the best-selling game, secretly based on his bad dreams. For a large portion of their eight months together, Brett travelled without her. This past week had been his first week off for a long time. This past week, Kat pushed for alone time. She convinced him to let her spend the night.

The proposal almost started an argument. Brett found one crack in their otherwise smooth relationship. He wanted to wait for marriage to consummate their bond and she did not. Kat maintained that being physical was necessary to a healthy love life. Brett felt that it was more important to wait. He remembered from his short time living in Karsten Field that cementing their love in the eyes of God would bring them true happiness.

Each time this discussion arose, Brett eventually won out. He worried that Kat stayed with him only for his money, since he did not cave in to more base desires.

He dressed before leaving the bedroom. Walking the hallway from the bedroom to the kitchen, sunlight streamed in through the wall of windows making him squint. Fresh snow on the roofs of neighboring buildings made it that much brighter. Brett looked out at the steam and smoke coming from the myriad of chimneys and exhaust pipes. Then he caught the reflection of a poster on the glass.

Barn Burners had become an overnight success. The poster displayed a battle-ravaged fire fighter. He looked attractive enough that millions of mothers would buy the game, but not so much to intimidate the millions of teenage boys that wanted to play it. Wearing a special ion water suit, the hero smashed through a barn door. Splintered wood and flames seemed to shoot out of the picture. An assortment of bad guys toppled and flew through the air behind the hero, launched by various explosions.

Brett came up with the concept after one of the earliest times he recalled having the nightmare. Maybe guilt inspired it, maybe not. Brett decided instead of being the one to start the fire, he wanted to be the one that stopped it. He devised a hero called Firefighter Rex that battled a nefarious organization known as the Arsonistas. Each level of the game sent Rex into bigger barns, more maze-like with increasingly dangerous hazards. Rex had to defeat the team of villains one at a time to save the barns, cities and even the world. Not nearly as violent as other popular video games and presenting ideals of bravery and determination, the game became an instant success.

Money came with that success, but it was not a motivator for him. Brett put most of the money back into his company and rewarded his two college friends that helped him develop the game. He bought a two-thousand square foot apartment in one of those renovated art districts and now turned his attention to trying to decide on a *Barn Burners* sequel or something different.

Before making his way to Kat and whatever she concocted for breakfast, Brett stopped at the thermostat. He lowered it from a sweltering eighty-three to a more reasonable seventy. He had a delicate internet server and three CPUs in his office that would not survive that kind of heat. Maybe this was another crack in their relationship? If they could not accommodate each other in a simple morning routine, what would a future marriage be like?

Not that marriage was on Brett's mind. He had a lot on it, but long-term plans in that department were low on the list. He liked Kat a lot. He loved her. All the same, he did not know if eight months was a long enough time to know her and then make the decision to marry her.

He did know someone whose opinion he valued. His father.

Allan Howarth had experience with marriage. Twice. Both times, Brett knew, only a short time passed from first glance to "I do". Maybe Allan's marriage to his first wife did not last, but it produced Brett and his sister, so it could not have all been in vain. His second marriage seemed to be a gift from God. Almost as if Mary was waiting for him, Allan embraced a new life. Now Brett had a younger brother and sister. To his knowledge, Allan and Mary never had a sour day between them in over ten years. If Brett could not go to his father for relationship advice, then he could at least count on him for spiritual advice.

"Did you turn the heater off?" asked Kat.

Brett walked into the kitchen, his bare feet unaffected on the warm tile. He said, "I turned it down. You do realize how much work I, uh we, could lose if one of my boxes overheats?"

Kat put her coffee cup on the counter. Brett saw no other sign of breakfast. Apparently, since she did not eat, she must have decided he did not need to either. Walking out of the room, Kat shot a few words at him like small knives, "Sometimes, I think you care more about your video games than me."

It hurt for her to say that. Brett stood, wounded, with an empty cup. He looked at his single-cup coffee maker. The empty pot looked back at him. Its open, pouting mouth would not console him. No coffee. No eggs. Not even a frozen toaster waffle.

Brett had not been back to Karsten Field since graduating college. He went for a few days to see his father and then his life took on a new direction. Worldly success meant less time for things like distant relatives. He made plenty of promises, and excuses, to go see both of his parents, but work kept getting in the way. Holding that empty cup, wondering what Kat might say next, Brett discovered he had no more excuses. If he could not keep a promise to himself, how could he ever keep a promise to the woman he thought he might marry?

He carelessly set the cup on the edge of the sink. Before he made it out of the kitchen, he heard it fall into the sink. From the multiple clinks, he knew it broke. Brett did not turn around; the cup had no sentimental value. He could not waste time and let the same thing happen to his relationship. He saw this moment as a tipping point. If he did not act, Brett knew his relationship could fall into the sink and he would be left picking up the pieces. He found Kat already dressed enough to be pulling on her furry boots.

"I thought we were going to spend the day together?" he started.

Kat gave a final tug at her boot and stood up from the bed. She said, "It's January and it's snowing. I'm going someplace where they use the heater."

Kat started to push past him. Brett could feel an angry wave emanating from her. He stepped in front of her, wanting to grab her shoulders. Katherina Verona already made a name for herself in the promotional arena at a young age. She did not get that reputation by being meek. Brett did not want to risk upsetting her, so he held his hands up like a crossing guard.

She stopped. Brett tried to give her a boyish grin and got a slight smirk in return that she tried to hide. He said, "Wait, please. I have an idea. Come with me today."

"Where?" she said, her aggravation seeming to subside into annoyance.

"I'm not going to tell you, but I can promise you will be back in time for work Monday morning."

Brett slowly lowered his hands and reached for her. Kat let him embrace her and she pressed her head against his chest. She said, "You know today is Friday?"

"Yeah, I know. It's going to take some time to get there. It will be good for us. It will be good for me, help me be a better man for you," he explained.

Getting packed and in the car, Kat showed amazing restraint. She did not ask once where they were going. Eventually, the curiosity must have gotten to her. Before they made it to I-80, the questions started.

"Are you going to tell me now?" she prodded.

Brett concentrated on the traffic zipping past him. For Friday noon, it seemed heavy. Maybe people were starting their weekend early, but there was no holiday. It should have been a normal Friday. He decided he did not need the extra distraction of her needling him about their destination, so he said, "We're going to see my family."

For a moment, he thought Kat might leap out of the car. He saw her hand involuntarily go for the door handle. In his mind, he pictured her doing a tuck and roll at seventy miles an hour. That would not end pretty. He gave a brief sigh of thanks when she did not yank the handle. He knew she had more sense than that.

"You're taking me to the commune?" said Kat.

"It's not a commune," started Brett.

Kat shifted in her seat to face him. She said, "You are basically kidnapping me and taking me to a cult."

He thought he saw a wry smile on her face, but wondered how serious she truly was. Brett said, "You don't know much about the Amish, do you?"

"Only what you told me," she answered. Brett caught a glimpse of the mile marker that told him they would be upon the wild curly-q interchange that led to the Indiana Toll Road and All Points

West. With potentially icy road conditions, Brett waited to respond.

Once clear of the loops and back up to speed, Brett said, "You know they're not a cult. They're my family. I know we've been having some difficulties lately and I want us to get back on track. I feel like if I can talk to my father and maybe old Mr. Zook; it will help clear my head. Amish have very high values when it comes to marriage."

Again, Kat seemed like she might jump from the car. She exclaimed, "Did you say marriage? I didn't say anything about marriage."

She looked like she went a little pale. Her dark bangs and short hair framed a nearly white face. Brett felt a surge of butterflies in his stomach as well. He had not intended to bring up that subject. In fact, it only ever came up on the few times that other topic arose and he insisted on waiting until after marriage.

When he felt like he could talk without passing out, Brett said, "I think we could talk about it. But I'm not asking, not right now."

Kat turned away from him. She stared out the window at the slushy, dirty snow blurring along the shoulder of the interstate. She said, "It's good that you're not asking right now. I don't know what my answer would be. I think you're right; we do have a lot to talk about. But not right now. I'm going to take a nap until we stop for lunch."

She scrunched down into her seat, but did not close her eyes. Brett could see the sparkling green of her fairy eyes reflected in the window. She added, "Will it at least be heated there?"

"The bed and breakfast has electric heat," Brett answered.

"I'm afraid that won't be possible." Ben Abrim Zook smiled as he delivered the bad news. He continued explaining to Brett and Kat, "Mr. Troyer has closed the bed and breakfast for the season since November last. He will not have sheets on the beds again until March at the soonest."

Brett turned to Kat as she shivered on the sidewalk. He tried to deliver his most apologetic expression. The uncomfortable car ride became that much more disheartening when they found out there would be no electricity. Brett survived well enough on his numerous visits, but he did not think Kat would stand for it.

"How close is the nearest hotel?" she asked. The look in her eyes told Brett that she wanted one in the direction of home.

"It's too late to get back out on the highway. We can stay with my dad," offered Brett.

Ben Abrim let out an exaggerated cough. He said, "Ahem, ahem. This is not something to be done either. We cannot allow an unmarried couple to share a bed in an Amish home. I would offer my spare room, but I already have house guests."

Brett pushed his glasses up toward his forehead and pinched his thumb and forefinger to the bridge of his nose. He used to only need glasses when working on his computer. Then he started wearing them behind the wheel. Lately, he sometimes forgot to take them off. He thought about his options and how best to make Kat happy. He said, "Mr. Zook, will it work if Kat stays at my dad's and I go stay with Alice and Sam?"

Ben Abrim removed his felt hat and rubbed the top of his balding head. "Well, as you said, no one is expecting you and it is a late hour. Only by God's grace did I find you here, as I needed to get formula for the baby. I think the sleeping arrangements will be acceptable if you don't mind walking alone to your sister's house. I will escort the young miss on my way home and speak with your father."

"Will that work?" Brett asked Kat.

"I've never met your family. I guess I will be cold and awkward," she said.

"Not at all," said Ben Abrim. "The schoolhouse has two woodstoves."

As Brett hiked down the moonlit path toward his sister's house, he only had his thoughts and the crunch of fresh snow to keep him company. It occurred to him that Ben Abrim mentioned a new baby. It seemed strange that the old man would be responsible for baby formula. He thought the midwives preferred natural feeding. At least they would have something to talk about in the morning.

While Brett wandered through the woods, Ben Abrim led Kat straight to Allan's door. They did not have to walk long, but Kat thought she might chip a tooth she was chattering so badly. She discovered Iowa was no better than Michigan in the winter. Cold is cold and she believed she would be quite happy on a tropical island. In fact, the only reason she stayed so long in Michigan was Brett.

They had a successful business venture together and she liked him. She would not admit to herself that she loved him. That did not mean she could not have fun with him. She received mixed signals when it came to that. He refused her advances, something unheard of among the girl gossip at work. This left her with doubt about how he really felt. She worried whether he thought she was beautiful. She worried if he could completely commit.

None of that mattered at the moment because she could barely feel her fingers or toes. For the icing on the frozen cake, Brett threw her into the lion's den. He left her alone to meet his family for the first time. To make it worse, he did not call them ahead of time to let them know they were coming. Sometimes, she liked Brett's spontaneity, yet other times it was one of his most annoying traits. If they were going to consider marriage, she would want him to demonstrate the ability to create and execute long-term plans.

Ben Abrim said nothing on their walk, but constantly looked at her and smiled. She wondered if he smiled like that all the time. A round face under a wide-brimmed hat, sporting a beard, but no moustache. Creepy, she thought. At least he has all his teeth.

The man that answered the door at the schoolhouse looked a lot like Brett. He had the same smile lines around his eyes and the same rust colored hair. He, too, sported a beard, except much longer than Mr. Zook's. She would know Brett's father anywhere.

"Mr. Zook, what brings you here at this late hour?" asked Allan, greeting his friend with a hug.

Kat saw a woman rising from a wide armchair in the room behind Allan Howarth.

Ben Abrim said, "I have brought you something to look after until morning. This is a good friend of your son's, Miss Katherina Verona."

Allan looked over the top of both her and Ben Abrim. Peering into the night, he said, "Is Brett here?"

His expression instantly switched from simple curiosity to anxious excitement. Ben Abrim brought focus back to Kat. He said, "Mr. Howarth, please. I have already sent Brett to stay with his sister, your daughter. I did not feel it would be appropriate for a friendly young couple to spend the night in your home out of wedlock. Miss Katherina is agreeable to staying with you."

Allan turned his attention to Kat. She felt like he suddenly accepted her as a substitute for his son. He said, "Where are my manners? Of course you are welcome." He wrapped his strong arms around her in a friendly hug.

From the doorway, Allan's wife called, "The child looks to be freezing. Bring her inside at once. I will make some hot apple cider while you, husband, move Benjamin from his bed. Brett's friend is welcome to share the bedroom with young Ruth."

Kat did not know what to expect, but she did not expect this. Ben Abrim left for his own home. Then these strangers brought her into their house with no questions. They showed her every hospitality as if she were a long lost family member. They did not riddle her with questions, but simply let her sit with a blanket over her shoulders and a delicious cup of cider warming her fingers.

A boy that obviously shared some parentage with Brett stumbled into the room. He looked like he could barely open his eyes for being so sleepy. "Who is this?" he asked.

"Benjamin, this is our new friend. Tomorrow's breakfast will be a better time for questions. I've moved you once, now back to sleep," ordered Allan.

By the time Mary showed Kat to Benjamin's recently vacated bed, Kat felt like she had known the couple for years. She could only say "Thank you", but she said it repeatedly.

Brett stood outside the familiar cabin for half an hour before going to the door. Mostly he stared at the barn. It was not the same barn and the generator, or what survived, had long been dismantled and hauled away to who knows where. Brett thought he might like to have a fragment of that dreaded machine. Maybe he could display one of the knobs on his office bookshelf.

Looking at the barn, Brett tried hard to remember what the old barn looked like. He knew the vision from his dream was a twisted version. That was the only image he could conjure though. Other than that, he could only remember the heat. It seemed, in his dream and waking memory, that the fire surrounded him immediately. He did not have a chance to react. He could remember heavy beams crashing down around him. Then he stood outside, not sure whether to fear the fire more or his father's reaction upon discovering him as the cause.

Brett never really wanted to be a part of Karsten Field. He never wanted to live here. He did not want to leave his father either. The barn incident made that decision for him. He went on to live with his mother and only came back to visit as a friendly outsider. He watched his father and his sister change. He saw happiness come into their lives that he never imagined possible. He was not unhappy, but he saw a peace in their lives that did not seem to readily exist in the outside world.

He wanted some of that peace and happiness in his life.

He thought Kat could bring that to him, but he needed a better understanding. He knew Karsten Field was a place of understanding. A candle igniting in the cabin window shattered Brett's thoughts. He watched the light float from what used to be his father's bedroom toward the front door. The door opened and a male voice called, "Who is going there? Come to the house before you are frozen in the snow."

When Brett came close enough to reveal his identity by candlelight, Samuel almost cheered loud enough to wake the twins. He pulled Brett inside and went to rouse Alice from bed. She greeted her brother with equal excitement. The three of them talked long into the night with the promise that Samuel would wake Brett early to take him to Allan on their sled.

And Samuel fulfilled his promise. Brett had not survived on such a small amount of sleep in a long time. He guessed maybe he got four hours of rest. Still, Samuel's eagerness was contagious. Brett dressed quickly and joined Samuel on the front porch.

Alice kissed her husband and said, "Come back for us soon, ja? I will dress the kids and then come help Mary make a fine dinner for us all."

Brett and Samuel found Allan waiting for them. He stood at the pass on top of the hill, leaning against the corner post of the footbridge built by Mr. Esch after the great flood. The strength of his father surprised Brett. The man, who he had not seen in almost three years, pulled him from the sled bench and hugged him fiercely. He squeezed his son and tears streamed from his eyes. Brett would remember this hug as one of the three best in his life. The other two were still in the future.

Samuel carried the father and son to the schoolhouse and left to gather his own family. Brett and Allan sat at the kitchen table while Mary started preparing breakfast.

"What do you think of Kat?" Brett asked.

"I think she is still sleeping," answered Allan.

Mary tapped Allan on the shoulder with her wooden spoon. She said, "That is not what he means, husband."

Allan rubbed his shoulder, feigning injury. He said, "I know what he means. Can a man not make a joke in his own house? To tell truth son, we did not speak much last night. It was our wish to meet her through your eyes. It is the beauty you see in her and the love that you have for her that matters most to us."

Those were the kinds of things Brett wanted to hear. Already he felt like coming to Karsten Field was the right decision. He had not seen his family in so long. He barely recognized Benjamin when the boy came into the room.

"He is a lot like you," Allan said to Brett as he pulled Benjamin onto his lap. "You cannot imagine my joy at reliving this part of life again. One of my greatest pleasures was always holding my children. God gave me that gift again when I thought I was too old."

Brett fidgeted in his seat. He had a specific question to ask his father and felt funny asking in front of Mary and Benjamin. He asked, "Can we go outside?"

"For what?" asked Allan. He must have seen the look on Brett's face because he added, "Say what you will in front of Mary. She is my wife; we are of one flesh, one heart and one ear. If you do not share it now, I will share it later. From the blush in your cheeks, I can guess where this is going."

Allan scooted Benjamin off his lap and the boy ran into the other room. Brett summoned the courage and hoped Kat would not wake up at this moment.

He said, "It is a question of..." He paused, cleared his throat. "I mean, she has certain expectations. Expectations that I am not ready to meet. I think it is important to wait for marriage."

Allan laughed aloud. Mary quickly turned to the stove so Brett could not see her face. Allan said, "Son, I am sorry. I am not mocking you. I laugh because it brings my heart joy to see you are the one that wants to wait. When I was your age, other guys looked at you funny if you were not out chasing girls."

"Gee, thanks," said Brett. He took a big drink of milk, hopefully to loosen his throat.

Allan reached across the table and held his son's hand. He looked him in the eye and said, "With seriousness, the Corinthians ask *do you not know that the unrighteous will not inherit the kingdom of God*? The matters of your heart are between you and God. You have to know, with or without this woman, if you will be with God. Saving yourself for marriage is an honorable thing and holy in the eyes of God. This flesh will turn to dust and what will you have to take with you after that?"

Those few words burned into Brett's heart. He felt the heat of them as sure as he felt the heat of the flames all those years ago. Allan had awoken something in him. Brett knew at that moment that he did want to marry Kat, if she would have him. He wanted to become one with her, but not only in flesh. He wanted to show her God's peace. He confessed to Allan and Mary that he was not going to move to Karsten Field, but that he would glorify God in all that he did in his life. The conversation turned to his work and how he could share God's message through video games. The talk lasted another hour and no one disturbed Kat until breakfast was fully ready.

Kat's eyes fluttered open.

She felt unbelievably comfortable and warm. Other than that, she noticed two things. First, she heard voices, Brett's and two others, talking excitedly in another room.

The other thing she noticed was a beautiful little girl sitting at the foot of her bed. The girl held a worn, faceless doll and looked like an angel from any of countless paintings. Kat realized this had to be Brett's youngest sibling, Ruth, who had been sleeping in the bed by the window last night.

Waking up in this strange house skewed Kat's perception. She felt a million miles away from her job and everyday life. She felt lighter, as if her frustrations and cares had been temporarily lifted from her shoulders. This place had an effect on her. She could not quite place the feeling, maybe it came from the people, or maybe it came from the land itself.

Ruth smiled at her. She said, "Good morning."

"Huh, oh, good morning," Kat murmured.

"Isaac wanted me to tell you something," said the little girl.

"Who's Isaac?" asked Kat. She was not awake enough to be honestly interested.

Ruth said, "He's my guardian angel. He says *for this is the will of God, even your sanctification, that you should abstain* and *he that overcometh shall inherit all things*. I don't know what that means, but Isaac said you would."

Then Ruth jumped down from the bed, whispered something to her doll and left the room.

Kat sat up in bed. She could not believe what she heard. What child talked like that? The words abstain and overcome seared her mind. She suddenly realized what she had been doing. Another word flashed in her head: temptation. She had been tempting Brett, but also herself. In love and relationships, Kat had no real experience. She pressured Brett to gain that experience without concern for his feelings or beliefs. She understood that if she truly loved him then his wishes would be hers. She never really considered herself a Godly person, but hearing God's words from a child's mouth did something to her.

Maybe, she thought, God saw her here. Maybe He saw someone that did not belong and someone that needed guidance. She wanted to talk to Brett about her realization, but the eight-hour drive back home might not be enough time for that. They would need to at least double that trip for everything Kat felt like she needed to say. Until they had that opportunity, she would enjoy their time together with his family.

Brett did not think Allan would stop talking. It had been several years since he last saw his father and the man had much to tell him. Brett could not keep it all straight, but it all seemed connected. First, they had a flood, and then a drought. Then an Amish African American family showed up to give them some money. Allan talked highly of a Miss Margaret and her paintings. He indicated that she and Ben Abrim had become quite good friends. Brett's imagination ran away with the thought that no one could explain how the paintings ended up in Margaret's attic.

"What is this about Ben Abrim and a baby?" asked Brett.

Allan rocked his chair back on two legs. He looked almost to fall over backward, but caught his balance at the last moment. He said, "That is a story you might not believe. According to our little Ruth, Baby Jesus himself was born in your sister's barn."

"That is a great story, but is Ben Abrim....?" Brett could not control the smile that spread across his face.

"Goodness, no," said Allan. "There is a young Hispanic couple that came to us either by accident or God's providence. Miss Margaret was to take them to a shelter in Des Moines, but they have so far been staying at Ben Abrim's house."

Mary stepped away from her skillet, leaving some of Mr. Gundy's bacon to sizzle and fill the room with a delectable smell. She interjected, "They speak almost no English and are not much for conversation. Yet, they are married and have a clear love of their child. From what we can tell, they have family down at Kansas City. If my husband agrees, I think I know how to get them now to their family."

Allan looked at his wife. Brett watched the unspoken communication that took place between them. He knew that a love truly blessed by God came with many benefits. On most things, Allan and Mary were of the same mind. Allan seemed to understand his wife without further discussion.

He turned to Brett and said, "Son, do you think you can deliver this young family down to Kansas City?"

"Not without breaking a promise," said Brett.

"What promise?" asked Kat from the door of the kitchen.

Dressed, but with unbrushed hair and no make-up, Brett thought she never looked more beautiful. He almost jumped from his chair as he went to her. Kat took a big step toward him and they locked in one of those unconditional, all-worries-aside hugs. She squeezed him like she had not seen him in years. She squeezed him hard like Allan did that morning.

After seeing the barn that haunted his dreams and the talk with his father this morning, Brett felt something new toward Kat. The way she held him, made him wonder what experience she had. He thought she might feel something too.

Kat whispered in his ear, so low that he could almost not hear her, "I want to wait."

Brett almost let loose of the hug, but then he lifted her and spun around with the laughter of Allan and Mary providing background music.

Kat's words meant that she decided to respect his wishes, but they meant something more. Brett understood that something followed the waiting. He understood that she wanted to marry him. What came after that was not nearly as important as the fact that she found God's virtue in one night.

In his memory and dreams, Brett felt like he idealized Karsten Field as a mystical place of miracles. Good things seemed to happen to the people there. He thought it was due to their closeness with God and a strong adherence to His plan. Brett never expected to share in one of those miracles, but he felt like he was now.

"I'm sorry I have to break my promise," he finally said.

"I heard you say that before. What promise?" said Kat.

Brett looked to Allan and Mary, then said to Kat, "I know I promised to have you back to work on Monday, but I think we are meant to do something else that will keep us on the road a while longer."

He prepared himself for Kat's disappointment. Instead, she smiled and said, "Good. That will give us time to talk. I have a lot on my mind about our future."

Our future. Brett liked the sound of that.

"We should tell Ben Abrim that you are going to deliver his friends," said Allan. "I will go after breakfast and you may come with me son. There are many friends who would be blessed to see you again."

Mary hugged Brett and then went to the living room. Brett heard her open one of the old drawers. She came back with a kapp, handed it to Kat and then hugged her as well. Mary said, "You will need this child. Tomorrow is our turn to hold church. I will like it much to have you sit next to me and Alice and Ruth."

After church, an abundance of food, and more hugs than Brett could count, Monday morning finally arrived. The new parents, Jose and Maria, filled Brett's backseat. They surrounded a baby safety seat that Miss Margaret procured from a thrift shop.

Brett and Kat said their goodbyes with promises to return much sooner. Then, instead of heading back east on I-80, they went west. Both Kat and Brett had a lot to say about their relationship and the joy they found in each other. Jose and Maria sat in the back, all smiles. Mostly, they cooed at their baby, Jesus.

Kat had one question that surprised Brett. He had no response when she asked, "Did you know your little sister has a guardian angel?"

CHAPTER SEVEN

THE FALL

Brett and Kat left only that morning. Already, Ruth missed them. She loved her older brother, but he was something of a mystery to her. It seemed strange to have an adult brother. She liked being close in age to Benjamin.

Brett offered a different feeling. The fact that he did not visit often made Ruth wonder where he went. Her Datt said Brett lived in the outside world. Most of the time, Ruth gave no thought to the outside world. This recent visit from her brother and his girlfriend sparked young Ruth's imagination. She envisioned the outside world to be both dangerous and exciting. She knew God provided everything they needed here in Karsten Field. That made her wonder what Brett needed outside of their home.

She worried about her big brother. In Ruth's mind, monsters inhabited the outside world. Isaac told her about monsters that wore men's faces. They committed sin for pleasure and delighted in hurting others. To any five-year-old, the thought of monsters would send them under the covers of their parents' bed. Ruth took it as a matter of fact. She had nothing to be afraid of because God held His hands over Karsten Field. Isaac told her so. The Lord protected them because they glorified Him in everything they did. Ruth knew an Amish home would be safe from monsters.

Isaac also told her that God had plans for Brett. She still worried about him going out and being surrounded by monsters. She worried that Brett did not clearly see God at work in his life. Brett had to go into the outside world and he might have to fight the monsters. At least he had Kat with him. Ruth liked Kat. She would not stand for any *funny business*, as her Mamm called it. Ruth believed Kat would help Brett stay on the right path. Maybe together, she hoped, Brett and Kat would share some of God's love with the outside world.

Ruth sat on the edge of her bed, brushing her soft brown hair when her father entered the room. He wore his work boots. Ruth watched to see if he would track mud into her bedroom. She knew he worked outside all day, getting ready for school to start again after the Christmas break. By this time next year, Ruth looked forward to joining her brother, cousins and the other children in school. Ruth stopped brushing as he plopped down next to her.

"Will you brush my hair?" she asked. Ruth especially liked her time with her father. She did not wait for an answer and handed him the brush.

Allan held the brush up and examined it. He said, with a surprised look, "This is more a job for your Mamm. I have a hard time brushing my own hair, what is left of it."

Allan removed his black hat and ran his fingers through his thinning hair. Ruth recalled him once saying he wished it still grew as well on top of his head as it did on his chin and in his ears. She stuck her tongue out at the thought of thick, bushy hair growing out of his ears.

Although he verbally refused, Ruth knew her Datt could not resist spending time with his daughter. He started brushing her hair, as he had many times before. He may have said it was her Mamm's job, but she suspected he liked doing it.

Then Benjamin burst into the room. From the doorway, he kicked his shoes off without unlacing them. When he flicked each foot, one shoe hit the wall near the foot of his bed and the other landed on his bed. Benjamin looked over and froze. The look of concern on his face told Ruth that he had not expected to find one of his parents in his bedroom. He hurriedly gathered his shoes and stacked them nicely by the closet. Then he quietly removed his shirt, folded it and placed it on top of his dresser. He did not say a word as he readied himself for bed. Ruth assumed he did not want to risk displeasing their father.

"Time to get under the blankets," Allan said as he stood. He put the brush on the children's shared dresser drawers and waited for Ruth to climb under her covers.

Ruth asked, "Datt, do you think Brett and Kat will get married?"

Allan stood over her bed. A big smile grew on his face. He put his hands on his hips and said, "Yes, I do at that."

Ruth liked his answer. She hoped her brother would marry Kat. Then maybe they could come to live in Karsten Field. More importantly, she asked another question. "Do you think they will bring me a new cousin?"

Her father looked like someone was tickling him. He seemed to want to laugh, but held it. He said, "That is a possibility. I would gladly welcome another grandchild, if it is the Lord's plan."

Allan kissed his daughter on the forehead. Then he turned to Benjamin's bed. The boy said, "Goodnight," and pulled the covers over his head before his father could kiss him. Allan started to leave the room.

The thought of having a new cousin stirred one more question in Ruth's head. Before her Datt could leave, she asked, "Where do babies come from?"

Allan did not move at first. Then he went to the lamp on the dresser. Before he extinguished it, he looked at his daughter and said, "Maybe that is a question for your Mamm. Ask her in the morning. Goodnight, mein herz."

The worst of winter passed and school started again. Ruth liked having the other kids around, but she also felt slightly excluded. Both of her parents focused on the school. She could not wait until the fall when she would start kindergarten.

The cold weather finally broke and the snow-covered hills turned to mud-covered hills. Ruth wanted to be outside. She wanted to walk with her Datt in the woods and play by the river when the men went fishing. However, a surprise storm gave them another ten inches of fresh snow. Ruth heard several of the adults remark how they thought winter was over and they had not expected any snow in March this year.

Maybe playtime would have to wait, but Ruth still got some outdoor time with her father. Allan took Ruth to visit Ben Abrim. They did not have far to walk, but it always felt like a great journey climbing that hill. Once they passed the footbridge at the top, Ruth could hear Mr. Gundy's pigs oinking playfully. She could see smoke coming out of the chimney pipes of the wood stoves in all of the houses. Everyone stayed nice and warm. Despite the blanket of new snow, Ruth did not feel that cold. The shining sun glinted off of the ice crystals. Ruth did not know the word for it, but it was exhilarating.

Allan saw Max Troyer go by their house on his sled earlier that morning. He headed in the direction of Kinzinger's restaurant. A short while later, he came back by with a passenger. Miss Margaret came for another visit with Ben Abrim. Since Christmas, Margaret's visits had become quite regular. She now came to Karsten Field at least three times per week. She and Ben Abrim spent a lot of time together.

Allan decided it was time for his own visit.

Ruth had been asking for some time outside, so Allan decided to take her with him. They did not bundle too heavily. The warm sun already started melting the unexpected snowfall. The short walk up the hill always sent Allan's mind back to the day of the flood. He had several moments in Karsten Field where he felt God's presence. That day was one of the strongest.

Ruth ran ahead, clomping her little boots on Ben Abrim's front steps. Snow splashed off in every direction. She turned back to look at him.

"Hurry up, Datt! Do you think Ben Abrim will have hot chocolate?" she asked.

"Miss Margaret is here, so it is likely he will have a chocolate fountain," Allan teased.

"Really?" marveled Ruth. Her mouth hung open in obvious disbelief. Allan could see a spark in her eyes. He guessed she was imagining what a chocolate fountain would be like.

"I'm sorry to disappoint you, mein herz. There will be no chocolate fountain. Go inside and give Miss Margaret a hug," said Allan.

He followed his daughter inside when Ben Abrim opened the door. Apparently, he heard them making noise on his front porch.

"Mr. Howarth, how good of you to come by," beamed Ben Abrim. He looked genuinely happy to see his friend. "And you brought my favorite young lady with you."

Ruth squeezed Ben Abrim. Allan liked how the two of them always had a special connection. Ben Abrim was as close to a grandfather as Ruth had. He seemed to take to the role with ease and delight.

Ruth asked, "Do you have hot chocolate?"

Ben Abrim smiled. His cheeks looked somewhat rosier than usual to Allan. Ben Abrim said, "As a matter of fact, Miss Margaret was about to boil some water. Maybe you should help her in the kitchen."

Margaret held out her hand to Ruth. Allan noticed a significant change in her over the past several months. It had been less than a year since her husband passed away. When they first met her, she seemed to have lost her vitality. Allan suspected she found it again in the company of Ben Abrim. He thought about how neatly God arranged things in Karsten Field. Everything always seemed to find its place. Allan would not be so rude as to ask Margaret her age, but he believed she was quite a bit younger than Ben

Abrim. In the end, it did not matter to him, as long as they were happy together.

On the way to the kitchen, Allan heard Ruth ask Margaret if they had a chocolate fountain. Margaret laughed at this and Ben Abrim gave Allan a quizzical look.

The older man shook off his confused look, replacing it with a stern demeanor. Once Margaret and Ruth walked out of earshot, Ben Abrim said, "I am quite confused."

"What have you to be confused about, old friend?" asked Allan. He had a guess, but waited for Ben Abrim to confirm it.

"It is Margaret."

Allan nodded his understanding.

Ben Abrim continued, "I believe we have become quite good friends. I have always been surrounded by such good family. In my heart, long ago, I accepted that I would be alone. The Lord took my wife home and left me with no children of my own. Then you and your family filled that space. You have become my best friend since Mr. Tunstile delivered that letter which brought us together. I never asked God for anything for myself, yet he provided more than I could ask. Now, he has brought Margaret into my life."

Ben Abrim pulled a handkerchief from his pocket. If it was possible, his cheeks looked even redder. He wiped some nervous sweat from his forehead.

"You have feelings for her?" prodded Allan.

After a deep breath, Ben Abrim said, "I do. I do not know how many years our gracious Lord has planned for me, but I would like to spend them with her."

"That is great news. Don't let it upset you so," said Allan. He slapped a hand on Ben Abrim's shoulder. His mind jumped to a double wedding for Ben Abrim and Brett. Too many details got in the way, but Allan would love to see his son and his good friend married on the same day. It had been too long since their last wedding. Allan's rational mind saw many issues blocking the possibility, but his heart cheered.

Ben Abrim gestured for Allan to lower his voice. Apparently, he was not ready for Margaret to know his feelings. He said, "You forget one thing from which none of us are exempt. She does not walk in the faith. No matter how I feel in my heart, I cannot go against the Ordnung."

Allan admired his friend for being earnest in his beliefs. Of everyone in Karsten Field, Ben Abrim followed the word as law. He kept faith and adhered to their Ordnung in the face of every adversity. One might say he would sacrifice his happiness for it, but Ben Abrim found his happiness in service of God. The physical world only held meaning for him in as much as how it would affect his spiritual journey. The old man would not risk his everlasting reward for even a moment's indulgence.

Allan had an idea. He said, "This is easily solved, Mr. Zook. All of us can see how you two are good for each other. Miss Margaret has found renewed life. You should ask her to renew her spirit."

"What are you saying, Mr. Howarth?"

"Ask her to be baptized and walk with you in God's light," finished Allan.

The answer seemed obvious and simple to Allan. However, Ben Abrim looked worse. His feelings for Margaret must have developed greatly. Allan usually saw behavior like this from teenage boys. He never expected Ben Abrim to be shaken to his roots.

"Would you like me to have Mary talk to her?" asked Allan.

Ben Abrim dabbed at his forehead again. He said, "No, no. I could not ask your wife to do such a thing. I will do it when the moment presents itself. I wonder if we should be alone together with these thoughts in my head."

It took great control for Allan not to laugh. Ben Abrim lived more than eighty years on this earth. They did not have to dampen the youthful fire of an adolescent spirit. The rules and intentions of the young did not apply in this case. No one had to guard against temptation if the two of them were left alone together.

Stifling his amusement, Allan said, "I think the time has presented itself. It won't be too many weeks until Ethel Kurtz's baptism. Why not do them both at the same time? Not many men are blessed to baptize their own wife."

Margaret and Ruth came back from the kitchen, putting an end to their conversation. The four of them drank their hot chocolate in an awkward silence. Allan and Ruth left when they finished their drinks. Allan reassured Ben Abrim that he was doing the right thing. Margaret must have heard him because she gave Allan a sideways smile. The happy glimmer in her eye told Allan that she would make a wonderful wife for his friend. He did not doubt that she would want to be baptized. When she discovered those paintings in her attic, it sent her on a path directly to Karsten Field. Allan knew that Ben Abrim would love and honor her until God called them home.

A few days later, the snow began melting in earnest. The weather warmed as a spring day should. Ruth felt the urge to be outside and Saturday morning could not come soon enough. The snowstorm knocked over an old tree near Alice and Samuel's house, so Allan went to help clear it now that they could stand to be outside without freezing.

That left Ruth to wander with her brother. Most of the time, they got along well. An adventure seemed to be exactly what they needed. Ruth even helped her mother make a pair of sandwiches so she and Benjamin could stay out all day.

"Do not go near the river," ordered Mary. "The water is not warmed yet and you will catch cold if you get wet."

Ruth asked, "Why is Datt chopping down perfectly good trees today?"

Mary finished wrapping the sandwiches in a white cloth. She explained, "The heavy snow weighed on some of the older trees. The dead wood could not stand it and fell over. Your Datt is not cutting any good trees. He is only clearing away the bad wood."

The answer satisfied Ruth. Then she did some ordering of her own. Benjamin had been taking his time getting dressed. She rushed him out the door so they could enjoy the sunlight and warm breeze. Naturally, his first stop was a mud puddle where the melting snow had been running down the hill. He splashed hard and sank in knee deep. Droplets of muddy water almost hit Ruth, but she ran away from her brother. She did not want to start the day soaking wet.

It took a full two minutes for Benjamin to climb out of the bog. When he did, he wiped his dirty hands on his coat. Ruth knew this coat was a hand-me-down from the Menlachs. She suspected Benjamin knew that too. He would not be so careless with clothes their mother made. Ruth wished he would have respect for all of his things. His behavior had not been the greatest lately. She worried her brother would be getting a switch soon. Then he might treat things nicer.

Since their mother told them to stay away from the river, Ruth led the way along the path behind the schoolhouse. She had been this way many times. The path wound through the woods at the bottom of the hill, which eventually led to

Ben Abrim's and the Gundy's. However, she did not want to go that way today. She wanted to go deeper into the woods. She wanted to be surrounded by the leafless trees and maybe see some animals. Ruth did not expect to find more than a few birds or squirrels. All the same, she would be happy to meet any of God's creatures. Secretly, she hoped to meet a deer.

As the snow melted, it revealed more of the familiar path. It looked like a wavy brown stripe on a mostly white paper. It reminded Ruth of the paintings that Ben Abrim bought from Miss Margaret. She wondered if the painter, Simon, felt like this when he painted. Everything looked clean and crisp. Then a line of color cut through the middle of it. The gray and brown of the tree bark mixed across the white canvas. It all seemed so perfect and made Ruth happy.

They did not usually take the back way to Ben Abrim's house. In the summer, bushes and poison ivy grew on the path. Today, they came to the turn where the path led uphill toward the back of Mr. Gundy's pigsty. Ruth looked left, up the hill, then she looked to her right. The snow pressed down on the bushes, inviting her to explore the waiting forest. In the distance, she caught a brief glimpse of the deer she eagerly wanted to see. It bounded off out of sight. Ruth decided immediately that she wanted to follow it.

"Let's make a new path," she said to her brother.

Normally, Benjamin did not like her ideas simply because they were not his own. It surprised her when he said without argument, "Okay."

Together, the brother and sister left the path and delved deeper into the woods. The warm sun stayed with them, unobstructed by the lack of leaves above them. A few trees showed signs of buds, but Ruth thought they would have to start over because of the storm.

After walking about ten minutes, Benjamin stopped and bent low. He gestured to Ruth to be quiet, by putting his index finger against pursed lips. Then he pointed at the ground. Ruth moved next to him without saying a word. When she was close, she could see that he pointed at deer tracks in the snow. This far into the woods, the snow had not really started melting yet. The row of tracks looked perfectly preserved on the white ground. Ruth looked in the direction the tracks led, hoping to see the deer that made them.

They waited silently for a few minutes. Apparently, Benjamin could not stand it any longer. He ran the same way the tracks led. Ruth looked back over her shoulder. For a moment, she worried about finding her way back to the path. The excitement of catching up to the deer overwhelmed her. She ran after her brother. Her wool cloak snagged on a branch and she yanked it free. She could barely keep up with Benjamin. The deep snow slowed her little feet.

Finally, Benjamin stopped in a small clearing. The white snow gave way to some yellow grass that had yet to begin its spring rebirth. They lost sight of the deer's tracks. Ruth stood, catching her breath. She looked all around her. She believed the deer had to be close. When she looked back at Benjamin, she found him climbing up the slanted side of a tree that leaned against its neighbor, a sturdy looking oak.

Ruth could not help the instincts instilled by her mother. She said, "Benny, you get down from there. Remember what Mamm said about the snow on the trees."

Benjamin looked down at her from what seemed like a great height. Ruth had no way of estimating it, but in reality, he was only about six feet off the ground. He climbed with both hands holding the trunk and walking with his mud caked boots. About every other step, he slipped because of the mud on the bare, wet tree. The bark had been worn off by weather or an animal. Ruth guessed the tree had been leaning like that for some time. Benjamin stood straight when he could reach the adjacent tree. He held on to the oak and stomped his feet on the fallen tree.

"See, it's stuck. Nothing is going to happen," said Benjamin.

"But Mamm said heavy snow makes old trees fall over," replied Ruth.

"This one is not going anyw..." started Benjamin. A cracking sound interrupted his words. The tree slipped once and then again. As the old tree dislodged itself from the side of the oak, Benjamin jumped clear. Ruth's small body had no time to react. The tree dropped down on top of her.

For a moment, everything went black. Ruth thought the tree fell on her head. Then she realized that her cloak had folded up over her. She pushed the wool out of her eyes and stared at the side of the tree, inches from her face. She tried to stand, but could not move.

"Benny!" called Ruth.

"I'm over here. I'm okay," he answered.

"I'm stuck," said Ruth.

She tried to move again. The fallen tree held her in place. She could feel her toes and did not have any pain. She must have sunk down in a drift of snow. Maybe the old tree hit another tree or rock that kept it from crushing her, she guessed. Even if she was not hurt, she could not get out from under the tree.

"I can get you unstuck," said Benjamin. He pushed hard against the trunk. Ruth could hear him grunting, but the tree did not move.

"It's not moving, Benny. My legs are getting cold," said Ruth.

Benjamin looked around and found the cloth with their sandwiches. He handed it to her and said, "Here. Eat this. I'm going to get Datt."

"Hurry," Ruth shouted after her brother. He ran off in what she thought was the right direction.

Without Benjamin around, the forest suddenly seemed a lot quieter. It also seemed scarier. Ruth honestly loved the woods and nature. She suddenly became aware that she did not like being alone in the woods. She tried to twist free. Maybe, she thought, she could catch up to Benjamin if she got free. It did not matter what she tried. The tree trapped her.

"Don't worry, Ruth. You're not alone," said a gentle voice behind her.

Ruth could not turn to see the speaker, but she knew Isaac when she heard him. It had been a while since she last saw him. He sat down next to her and she looked into his steel blue eyes. They seemed to change color with the weather. In the summer, his eyes always seemed deep blue like the river. Now, they looked like something between the snow and the sky.

"Can you get me out, please?" asked Ruth.

Isaac shared a comforting smile. He held up his hands, almost in a shrug. He said, "In my condition, I'm afraid I can't do much more than keep you company."

Ruth pushed against the wood again. Then she tried to relax. She said, "I'm glad I'm not alone."

"Even when I'm not here, you know you're not alone. Our Father is always watching. He may not make his presence known, but he is there. Sometimes, we have to make our own mistakes so we can learn and grow," said Isaac.

Ruth thought about his words for a moment. As she thought, she admired the shiny buttons on Isaac's green coat. His uniform always looked freshly pressed and clean. He never seemed to pick up any dirt or mud. The weather never affected his smooth hair either. Ruth noticed he was not wearing his metal hat today.

After thinking a moment longer, Ruth wondered aloud, "What mistake did I make? I wasn't the one climbing the tree. It wouldn't have fallen if Benjamin wasn't climbing on it."

Isaac looked up to where the tree had been leaning not too long ago. He said, "When you truly accept our Father, you accept that everything, good or bad, happens according to His will. When I used to travel, I saw things that I did not believe God would allow. Men hurting other men, women and children. After everything I learned growing up about being Amish and walking a righteous path, I could not understand why He would let the rest of the world fall so far."

Isaac paused. Ruth guessed he must have seen the confused look on her face. She did not really understand what he was saying. She had a sense of it though. She understood that sometimes things happened that she did not like or want. That did not mean that they were not supposed to happen. In the end, she knew she had to trust God.

It seemed like quite a while to Ruth that they sat in silence. Neither spoke. They only stared into the woods. At some point, a deer came close enough that she could almost touch it. She wanted to pet it, but she did not want to startle the creature. She looked to Isaac for what to do. He looked from her to the deer and nodded. Ruth reached up to pet the animal, but it jerked its head as if it was frightened. The deer scanned the woods and then sprinted in the opposite direction.

Isaac looked in the same direction as the deer. He said, "For one so young, you have great wisdom. I have to go now. Your family is coming. Don't worry, I think we will be together soon."

As Isaac stood to leave, Ruth asked, "You will come to visit me soon?"

"I don't think I can visit you again," Isaac started. He bit his lip. Ruth thought she saw tears in his eyes. He turned away and walked off as she heard others approaching. It did not make sense to Ruth. She wondered how she and Isaac could be together if he was not coming back.

The sound of Benny shouting "This way" kept her from finishing the thought.

Before she knew what was happening, her brother-in-law Samuel and Eli Gundy lifted the dead tree off of her. Her father pulled her out of the snow and squeezed her tight. Like Isaac, he looked like he wanted to cry.

"Why do you test my heart so? Are you hurt? How are your legs?" Allan bombarded her with questions.

Ruth repeated, "I'm fine. I'm fine."

The young men dropped the tree. This time, it thumped solidly on the ground. Ruth looked and saw nothing, no rock or other tree, that should have held it up. To the best understanding of her young mind, she should have been crushed. She had no explanation why she was not.

"Are you okay, sis? I'm sorry I didn't listen to you," said Benjamin.

"It's okay. Isaac kept me company," she answered.

Her father looked at her curiously. Then he hugged her again and they started the journey back home.

At home, Allan watched Mary bathe their daughter. He watched his wife check her twice for any sign of bruises or broken bones. He felt great relief and gave thanks that Ruth showed no sign of injury. A fall like that could have been serious.

Mary decided it would be best for both children to get some extra rest. After an early supper, she put Ruth and Benjamin to bed. Mary found Allan in the front room, preparing to leave.

"Where are you going, husband? The Lord has tested us this day. We should stay home and pray on it," she said.

Allan looked at his wife. Her face showed signs of their ten years of marriage, but she looked every bit as beautiful as she ever did. He knew she was right. For whatever reason, it seemed God used Ruth to test them over and over. She always seemed to be at the center of some commotion or concern.

He said, "As always, wife, you are right. I will not be gone long. I need to speak with Mr. Zook about our daughter. His words are often good council."

"Be back before dark, please," Mary said. She kissed her husband and straightened his hat, before seeing him out the door.

Allan did not waste any time getting to Ben Abrim's house. It took some self-control not to run. Still, he felt slightly out of breath when he knocked on his friend's door.

The small man who always smiled swung open his door. He said, "Mr. Howarth, I am happy to see you. I have some good news."

"And I think I can guess and it does my heart good. I have some news and some questions for you," Allan said.

Ben Abrim pulled the door wide and gestured to Allan. He said, "Come in so we can talk."

As Allan suspected, Ben Abrim's news had to do with Miss Margaret. It turns out that she shared similar feelings with Ben Abrim. The two of them were of the same mind regarding marriage. The only disappointing news Ben Abrim had was that she wanted to wait until the following spring.

"She said she has a few things to get in order. She is more than willing to take the vows and be baptized Amish. Her feeling is that the extra time will allow her to make the necessary adjustments," explained Ben Abrim.

"Praise the Lord," said Allan. It made him happy to see two good people come together and share God's glory. He felt his friend deserved some simple happiness at this point in his life.

Then Allan proceeded to tell Ben Abrim of Ruth's adventure earlier that day. He said, "I thank God that I did not find her lifeless under that tree. She said one thing that bothered me. She said Isaac kept her company. Mostly, I have dismissed her talk of him as an imaginary friend, but what if it is possible?"

"What is possible?" repeated Ben Abrim.

"Is she seeing an angel? Do you believe Isaac Karsten is her guardian angel?"

Ben Abrim leaned back in his rocking chair. He did not rock forward, but held his position. Candlelight flickered across his face. It seemed to Allan a long time before his friend answered.

Ben Abrim said, "I have witnessed God's presence many times in my life. Our Lord works in ways that we can never truly understand. I personally have never seen an angel. At least not in the sense of a winged being coming down from heaven. The angels I know are flesh and blood here on earth. People like you, Mr. Howarth, that never think of themselves and always put the needs of others first. They risk their own well-being to help their fellow man. To me, those are real angels. Everything else is God showing himself to us and letting us know of His reward in the next life."

He stopped talking for a moment and rocked back and forth. The chair gently squeaked on the wood floor. Ben Abrim continued, "I believe the good Lord has His hand on our young Ruth. Maybe she thinks she sees Isaac Karsten. As you say, I believe he is nothing more than an imaginary friend that helps her make sense of things that our minds take for granted or ignore."

Allan left Ben Abrim with his heart feeling a little lighter. He himself had witnessed the unexplainable. He never acted so arrogant as to say he understood God's plan in all that had happened to him. He knew Ruth was special. Everyone that met her felt the same. It made sense that her *guardian angel* was an imaginary friend. He did not want to risk blasphemy by claiming a spirit, other than God, walked beside his daughter.

When Allan got home, he asked his wife if the children were still awake. He wanted to tell them goodnight.

"I think Benjamin is feeling guilty," she said. "That is the sign of a good heart, but it has made him sleepy. Our little Ruth is still awake. She was asking for you."

Allan walked quietly to the children's bedroom. If Ruth fell asleep, he did not want to wake her. From his comfortable spot in the doorway, with the door cracked, Allan could see Benjamin's feet poking out from under his blankets. He eased the door open and it creaked slightly.

"Datt, is that you?" called Ruth in a loud whisper.

"It is," he replied. Allan tiptoed into the room. He sat on the edge of Ruth's bed. From the light of the setting sun spilling through her window, he could see her sleepy eyes. It must have taken great effort for her to stay awake, he thought. He pushed a wispy strand of hair out of her face. She shivered at the cold touch of his hand.

Allan continued, "It was a big day today."

"Benny took a long time to get you, but Isaac stayed with me," said Ruth.

"I wanted to ask you about your friend. Is he here now?"

Ruth shook her head rapidly from side to side.

"I know you talk about him sometimes. I have never asked, but I think I would like to meet him. Is that possible?" said Allan.

"I don't think you can see him," said Ruth. Then she yawned and stretched enough to make her whole body shake.

Allan bent to kiss his daughter on the forehead. He said, "We should talk more about Isaac in the morning. It is time that I had a better understanding of your friend. Goodnight."

Mary waited patiently in the front room. She looked to have a hundred questions for him. Allan did not know if he had the energy to answer them all. He did know, however, that a good hug from his wife would go a long way to calming his own nerves.

As they silently embraced, Allan heard the pad of little bare feet coming down the hall. He turned to see Ruth, in her nightgown, standing in the doorway.

"What is the matter, child?" asked Mary.

Ruth put her hand on her head, mimicking the way her mother might check for a fever. She said, "I don't feel good."

The next several seconds seemed to last forever and would play over and over in Allan's mind in the coming days and months.

He watched Ruth's eyes roll up into her head. He could only see the milky whites until her eyelids closed shut. Ruth's head lolled back. Her body convulsed. Allan could not equate the feeling to anything in his life. The pain of watching the inexplicable happen to one of his children reached into the core of his being. He felt his own knees unhinge, but he remained standing. It seemed that Mary started crying instantly. At once, Allan felt completely empty, yet burdened with an immense weight. It only became worse as he watched what came next.

The fall.

Ruth collapsed. She dropped like a heavy clump of snow falling off the eave. Allan watched her knees fold under her and saw her cheek bounce off the floor. His daughter did not make another sound.

CHAPTER EIGHT

REST ON GRACE

Allan watched the event over and over in his head. He saw Ruth fall, trapped in a moment of time that surpassed all of his memories. His heart beat loud in his ears, the beats seemingly thumping minutes apart. He could feel it in his chest too. He felt both a constriction and pounding. His heart wanted to beat its way out of his body, while his lungs seemed to seize. The sensation sank with a leaden weight to his stomach.

The pain, the knowledge, that he watched his daughter die bored into him. He felt it in his stomach as sure as if one of the strapping Troyer boys punched him. Not that they ever would hit anyone, but Allan thought of their arms like sledge hammers.

The twisting weight caused his knees to flex. If he could not find some inner strength, Allan would collapse as suddenly as his daughter did. In his head, he called out, "Father, please give me clarity."

Next to him, Mary made no sound. She did not move, did not even change her expression. Allan knew that his wife had no understanding of this moment. It was not like the time Brett broke his arm, or when Benjamin tried to do the same. This was no accident. For no apparent reason, their young daughter, who seemed touched by God, dropped to the floor dead before their eyes.

Allan knew with certainty that she was gone. For that reason, he did not panic. He did not run to his child. He believed there was nothing for him to do. Maybe it happened because she was outside in the snow and mud too long. Maybe she caught some kind of cold. Instead of feeling angry, Allan released his emotions to God. Maybe it was because of her guardian angel. Allan wondered if her connection to Isaac caused her to be taken so soon.

Allan concentrated hard on taking the steps that moved him across their wood floor. He knelt, deliberately lowering himself as not to fall. Behind him, Mary still did not move, only tears streamed down her cheeks. He would address his wife in a moment. First, Allan wanted to take care of his daughter. He placed his calloused hand on Ruth's warm cheek.

"She breathes," he half-whispered.

Allan's quiet words must have pulled Mary from her shock. She asked, "What did you say, husband?"

"I said she breathes," Allan repeated. Tears flowed uncontrollably from his eyes. He felt himself smiling. He felt her breath when he touched her cheek. Allan held a finger under her nose to convince himself. He pressed his ear against her chest and could hear the soft rhythm of her heartbeat. "Thank you, Father. Thank you, Father."

Mary dropped to her knees, startling Allan. He thought maybe the scare caused her to faint. He turned to find her praying. Allan understood her emotion. He knew if God wanted to bring his child to Him then so be it. At the same time, he did not want to lose his daughter.

Allan scooped Ruth from the floor and carried her to her bed. Mary followed, lighting candles which woke Benjamin. None of the commotion awoke Ruth.

"What's happening?" asked a bleary-eyed Benjamin.

As Allan wrapped Ruth in her blankets, Mary went to comfort Benjamin. She said, "Your sister has taken ill. We are going to sit with her for a while. Please try to sleep."

Benjamin put his head back on his pillow and closed his eyes. Throughout the night, Allan would catch his son staring at Ruth. He had never before seen the boy so concerned for his sister. He did not move, nor did he attract the attention of his parents. He kept a vigilant watch and did not sleep.

Mary brought several cold dishrags from the kitchen. She laid one across Ruth's forehead and used another to pat her cheeks. Ruth did not respond as if she had a fever. Allan wondered if some food did not agree with her. However, he never heard of an upset stomach causing someone to fall like that. Something touched his daughter and almost took her from him.

In the hours before dawn, Allan sat at Ruth's bedside, reading from his Bible. He read of righteousness and faith in the book of Romans. Allan worried that he was too self-righteous. He worried that he wanted to keep Ruth alive against the Lord's will. Allan felt a connection to God in Karsten Field that he had never felt before in his life. Ten years passed and he never doubted what God put before him. More than any of his children, Ruth challenged him. She challenged his beliefs. Allan wondered about her encounters with Isaac. He recalled her part in many of the great trials of his life: the flood, the drought, almost losing her at the auction. Maybe, he thought, she had been sent to be a test of Allan's faith. Maybe he became complacent and the Lord blessed him and his wife with Ruth. If God wanted to take her back, that would be the ultimate test for Allan. He admitted to himself that he did not know if he was strong enough for a blow like that.

Allan flipped the page. In chapter three, he read that *all have sinned and all fall short of the glory of God*. The words spoke to his doubt. He knew he was not perfect, but sometimes he let himself think he was living a perfect life. He knew complacency could lead to hubris. When he came to Karsten Field, Allan had been set free. He was not only freed from a life of materialism and sin, but he was also freed from doubt, worry and fear. As everything moves according to God's plan, why do I have fear now, he asked himself.

He continued reading, looking for an answer. Then something happened. Allan heard a familiar voice, but it did not come from the next room or outside. It seemed to come from inside his own head, or maybe his heart. He had not heard that voice in many years, but he knew to listen. The voice spoke the words that waited under his finger on the page, "That is why it depends on faith, in order that the promise may rest on grace and be guaranteed..."

Allan almost dropped his Bible. He received the clarity for which he prayed and he wept.

Mary found Allan asleep in the chair next to Ruth's bed. He had not left her side all night. She saw Benjamin peeking from under his covers. Obviously, he had not slept. She could not be angry at his disobedience, as it warmed her heart to see such compassion between siblings.

Mary took the Bible from Allan's lap and placed it on the dresser. She blew out the candle and pulled back the curtain to allow in the pink morning light. She had done her own praying during the night and managed to sleep a few hours. She knew her husband to be a man of determination. It would not serve a purpose for both of them to sit awake. Mary would let Allan care for Ruth, so that she could run the house and feed her family.

"Mamm?"

Ruth's voice startled Mary. She had already found peace that her daughter would be cradled in the arms of the Lord. Her heart would be satisfied even if she never heard Ruth's voice again. That is why she did not expect to feel so much joy when her daughter spoke.

"Husband, wake up. Your daughter calls," she said, shaking Allan's shoulder.

Mary sat on the edge of Ruth's bed. She asked, "What is it, mein herz?"

"My head hurts," said Ruth.

Allan sat up at the sound of her voice. He looked happy, but confused.

"Does anything else bother you?" asked Mary. Working with children most of her life, she never saw one collapse the way Ruth did. She had seen plenty of fevers and upset stomachs in class, and plenty of fakers. She prayed that whatever bothered her daughter would pass with some rest and hot soup.

"Only my head hurts. It makes me sleepy," answered Ruth.

Mary stood. She said, "Then rest now. Benjamin, come eat your breakfast. I will bring you some soup a little later. Husband, come talk with me."

"Would it be okay for me to eat breakfast here?" Allan asked.

"Husband, as long as we have been married, do you not know what to do when your wife gives you instructions?"

Allan followed Mary without another word. She knew he wanted to stay by their daughter. She wished she could do only that as well. At the same time, she did not want to discuss any of her concerns in front of the child. Besides, Allan still had chores to do. Ruth was awake with what seemed like nothing more than a headache. Sitting by her bed would not change that.

Mary followed Benjamin to the kitchen and served him the eggs she had scrambled. Then she ushered her husband into the next room.

"It would be a wise choice for you to go ask Alice to help with school today. None of us slept much and we can rely on our family and neighbors for extra help," started Mary.

"What of Ruth?" asked Allan.

"I know nothing like her symptoms," said Mary. "Let her rest for now. Maybe some sleep will help her get the bug out of her system."

"Then there is nothing more for us to do?" asked Allan.

"Nothing, except to wait with patience and see what will come of this."

Allan seemed reluctant, but he left the house to go speak with Alice. Mary made chicken noodle soup from an old recipe and noodles from Mrs. Kinzinger. By supper, Ruth wanted to run around with her brother. Each day after, Ruth got out of bed earlier until she was back to her old routine. Mary, nor her husband, would forget the *fall*, but life continued.

Something glorious happened in Karsten Field each April. Spring started and flowers bloomed. It seemed that every Karsten wife knew in advance when the weather would change. On the same day, presumably without notifying each other, these women would open their houses and clean out the winter dust.

At the Howarth house, and many others, that meant no young children under foot. The older children had plenty of chores. Ruth happened to be the youngest girl in Karsten Field, which excused her from some of the more challenging tasks.

Today, Ruth accompanied her father to visit Ben Abrim. That suited her fine. She would do her best to help her father. Ruth had every intention of being useful. She did not think being small was a good excuse for not being helpful. That, of course, did not include any opportunity to have fun. She knew her father would understand the need for some playtime.

Her playtime came after they left Ben Abrim's house. Her father said they needed to stop in at Mr. Gundy's.

Allan joked, "I need to see a man about a pig."

Her father said that almost every time they went to Mr. Gundy's house. Ruth did not understand it, but it made her smile.

Ruth ran over to the pigpen when her dad climbed the Gundys' front steps. Her small feet fit nicely in the rectangular spaces of the wire mesh. In a moment, she climbed up to the top and leaned over to watch the animals. Ruth pressed her thumb against the tip of her nose, exposing her nostrils.

"Oink, oink," she called and then giggled as the pigs grunted. She assumed they were talking only to her. She could not hear their continuous grunts from her house and thought they only made noise when she visited. If she heard the sounds they made at night, she might not think it was so funny.

A pair of hogs rooted in the corner on the far side of the pen. Ruth wanted to see them closer. One had large brown spots on its backside. She liked to imagine drawing lines between those spots to see what shapes she could make. Since she could not see them well, Ruth pulled herself up to the top of the fence. She balanced both feet on the four-inch space of the square post.

The new height did not provide a better view, so Ruth decided to walk along the narrow rail to the next post. She stuck her arms out to her sides and took the first step.

"Who do you think you are? Dorothy Gale?" called her father from Mr. Gundy's front porch. Ruth broke her concentration to look up at her father. It made her glad to see that he was not angry with her for climbing the fence.

"Who's that, Datt?" Ruth asked, turning her focus back to her feet. She stuck her tongue out the side of her mouth for added concentration.

"She's from an old movie," started Allen. He stopped short and Ruth looked up at him. His expression looked like he was keeping a secret from her. They played this game before and it usually ended in her being tickled. She did not want to be tickled at this particular moment. She guessed she needed only three more steps to the next post. Still, she wanted to know the secret.

"Will you take me to see a movie?" Ruth asked her father.

Allan turned from Mr. Gundy and started down the stairs. He said, "Maybe it will be better to ask your Mamm to read the book to you."

Ruth had heard her father talk about movies once before. She also heard Brett and Kat when they visited. The idea of giant people moving on a huge wall enticed her. Ruth tried to imagine what it would look like and closed her eyes.

Instead of seeing the talking giants, all she could see were stars. They did not look like the normal stars at night. She could see bright pins of light in the darkness. Some of the pins exploded into sparkling clouds. Ruth wanted badly to open her eyes. These stars scared her. It scared her more when she discovered she could not open her eyes. She felt suddenly dizzy and knew she was tumbling off the top of the fence.

In the distance, it sounded really far, Ruth could hear Mr. Gundy shouting, "She has fallen into the sty."

Another voice that sounded like her father yelling to her under water cried, "Ruth, I'm coming, Ruth."

Ruth could feel the cold mud envelope her body like a soft blanket. Then she went numb. She could no longer feel her hands or legs. She could not feel her body splat in the wet pigpen. She could not feel her head thump against the ground. She wanted desperately to open her eyes, but could only see those frightening, bursting stars. The voices around her sounded further and further away, continuously becoming quieter.

Then, nothing.

Those cold, cold feelings would not leave Allan's heart. He stood by as Mary bathed their child. He watched his wife wash the mud from Ruth's feathery brown hair. The whole time, Ruth did not wake.

Only an hour before, Allan watched his daughter tiptoeing her way along Mr. Gundy's fence. Allan watched her do it more than once. Maybe she did not know he watched, but he saw her. It was his responsibility. The father always watches.

Allan wondered what his Father could see now. He wanted to ask God why this was happening. He would not be one to challenge the Lord's will, but he could not understand it. Allan knew understanding was not always a necessity. Many things happened in his own life that he did not understand. Until this day, he always found those things to work for his good and to serve the glory of God. There seemed to be no good outcome for his daughter's condition.

Carrying her from the bathtub to her bedroom, Allan stared at Ruth's pale face. Her eyes fluttered open and Allan felt his heart miss a beat.

"I love you, Datt," she said.

Barely able to speak, Allan replied, "I love you, mein herz." He could feel a tightness in his throat and sweat on his palms. He thanked God if those would be the last words he heard from his daughter. Awake now, Allan had no idea if she would slip away during the night. Twice now, Ruth inexplicably fainted. No one in Karsten Field had any ideas or suggestions.

Once they had her tucked in bed, Allan spoke privately with his wife. He said, "There must be something more we can do."

"What does your heart tell you, my husband?"

Allan tugged at his own beard, as if the stinging follicles might ignite something in his brain. It sometimes surprised him how long the hair grew throughout his years of marriage to Mary. Most of his life, he had no beard and every once in a while, when lost in thought, he could not feel it.

Finally, Allan said, "My heart and my head are in agreement. It may be God's will to call her to Him, but it may also be His will that we seek help. I think, for our daughter, we must take action and not wait for something to happen."

"I will speak my mind on this," started Mary. "Normally, I would say *let it pass*. In my years of teaching, I have seen many strange behaviors from children. This is like nothing I have seen. I can look in your eyes and hear the sound of your voice, husband. If you have decided to take our child to an English doctor, then I am in agreement with you. I believe we know one or two that are friends of the Amish."

"That is good. I will ask Mr. Kinzinger for the money to pay the doctor," said Allan. He felt some relief in their decision. He did not risk breaking the Ordnung, but it felt better having the support of his wife.

Allan showed a confident face to Mary. He chose not to reveal his hesitation. His feelings for his young daughter clouded his beliefs. He had great faith that led him to this point. Now, he had feelings of doubt and selfishness. Allan believed God would protect his family because they did not live with the sins of sloth and greed like so many English. He found himself turning to those same English to help his daughter. He did not think of it as putting his faith in English medicine, but rather, he believed God could work through the hands of a healer. Maybe, he reasoned, their actions would be as much for Ruth as they would be for the English. Maybe Allan could show another lost soul the way to salvation.

Four weeks and three hundred dollars brought Allan no closer to an answer. Ruth fainted twice more in that time.

The first pediatrician suggested it could be seasonal allergies and wrote a prescription for a decongestant. Allan knew the doctor was wrong. He believed this was part of what was wrong with the English that he left behind long ago. This man saw that they had no insurance, which meant he had no way of making long-term money. He dismissed them out of greed. If Allan had the time or resources, he told himself he would sue that doctor for malpractice. Then his calmer head prevailed. Allan realized that it was not his place to seek vengeance.

The second doctor, a young woman and recent graduate named Wilson, at least gave them hope for an answer. Their lack of medical insurance also limited what this doctor could do, but at least she did not send them on their way. Doctor Wilson wanted to run tests, expensive tests, with initials like CT and MRA. Allan did not feel that this doctor was being greedy. He knew the English system was more about profit than health. The doctor did her best with what she could.

Without the conclusive tests or even, as she called it, a basic ultrasound, the compassionate woman told Allan and Mary that she could only guess what might be causing the fainting spells.

Leaving Mary and Ruth in a separate room, Dr. Wilson said, "Based on what you have told me, I worry that we might be looking at an aneurysm. I would not normally jump to this conclusion, but you mentioned the hallucinations."

"I did not call them hallucinations," corrected Allan. During the exam, he felt compelled to tell Dr. Wilson about Ruth's friendship with Isaac. He knew Ruth had insight that he never would. He reasoned that sharing this with the English doctor might help her on her own path.

Dr. Wilson said, "I'm sorry. If no one else saw this Isaac, then I have to rationalize it as a hallucination. It is not too common, but cerebral aneurysms can cause both fainting and hallucinations. I don't think we are talking about a rupture, but at her age and activity level, I recommend finding a way to get help."

Help.

Such a little word never seemed so daunting to Allan. With his every breath, help came from the Lord. For more than ten years, he had no worries that were not answered. Most of his life he lived in a secular world. Watching Ruth suffer brought thoughts and behaviors rushing back from that old life.

In the privacy of his bedroom, Allan let anger overtake him for a moment and he wept. Usually, he awoke at the same time as his wife. This morning, he could hear her already in the kitchen. For some reason, she left him asleep. With the rising sun, tears streamed down his cheeks, getting lost in the bramble under his chin.

He could barely speak between convulsions, but he prayed, "God, I don't know what to do. I know You have always had Your hand on our precious Ruth, but I don't believe You are ready to take her." Allan shuddered. At the same moment, his tears dried. He put his hands to his head and fell back on his pillow. He realized how wrong he was and said, "Here I am."

Allan's voice dropped to a whisper. He repeated, "Here I am." Allan understood that his daughter had the illness, but he was the one suffering. He had given his life to God, but like Abraham, Allan needed a test. It occurred to him that God was testing him now, pushing his faith to the limit, asking the ultimate sacrifice of a parent. "I was wrong," he whispered.

Allan had come to his own Jehovah-jireh and almost failed the test. The Lord asked Abraham to sacrifice his son Isaac and Abraham passed his test. Allan saw the irony in Ruth's guardian angel sharing the same name. It did not matter what Dr. Wilson said about the hallucinations, Allan knew the truth now. He became calm. His body relaxed. Allan said, "Father in Heaven, I give her up to you. She is of my flesh, but only You can deliver her spirit."

Something seemed to move past Allan's window. Allan jumped from bed and peered into the early morning light. It looked like someone was walking away from the house. It looked like a young man in a military uniform. Allan lifted the window to get a better look. Cool air smacked him in the face, sending a shiver down to his bare feet. He rubbed his eyes and took a second look. He saw no one.

For no particular reason, Alice and the twins came for breakfast. She said, "After I fed Samuel, it seemed like we should have a family visit. I wanted to hear news of Ruth and Samuel said better to go early."

Allan looked at his oldest daughter. She had grown into a fine woman and mother. He remembered a time not so long ago when he felt like he was losing her. Alice never faced a life-threatening illness. She was in danger of losing her soul to reckless behavior and vice. Karsten Field set her free too.

After hearing about the possible aneurysm, Alice asked, "I wonder why you have not talked to my mother?"

"We only learned of this yesterday. What could Tina have to say?" responded Mary.

"Her husband is a neurologist," said Alice.

Allan marveled at God's great works. No sooner had he offered up his daughter to his Lord's will, then a new possibility was set in front of him. He could not believe that the man his ex-wife met at a bible study group might be able to help Ruth. It seemed that it was Alice's purpose to deliver this news, foregoing the duties of her own house.

After breakfast, Alice and the kids went home. Allan skipped his own chores. With a supportive nod from Mary, he headed toward Kinzinger's restaurant to call Tina.

Allan kept Tina's phone number and address on a folded up piece of paper in the hall desk drawer. He kept it in case there was ever news of Alice or the grandchildren to deliver. Allan never found himself wanting to call Tina and visit about old times. They parted as friends, but shared nothing more after that than the lives of the two children they created. Tina was not a big part of Alice's life in Karsten Field because she moved away with her husband. Allan knew they talked occasionally, but Tina rarely came for a visit.

The phone call would be difficult. It seemed strange that Allan would have to go to Tina for help.

In a way, he felt she led him to Karsten Field in the first place. If they had stayed together, he would not be standing in this spot right now. The plastic receiver felt slippery in his sweaty hand. He noticed Mrs. Kinzinger leaning in from the kitchen window, so he turned his back to the service counter. The restaurant was small enough that he would have no privacy. Allan did not intend to speak any secrets, so it did not matter whether the restaurant was full or empty. This morning, it was empty though.

Ring.

Allan's heartbeat quickened. He had not had nerves like this in a long time. It felt strange to call his ex-wife.

"Hello?"

Allan almost stuttered, "Ja, it's me, Allan."

"Allan? Is everything all right? It's six-thirty in the morning here." The female voice sounded strange to Allan. It had been a long time since any female other than his wife Mary called him by his first name. He thought it was funny how a little thing like that can change your perceptions.

"I'm sorry. I forgot about the time difference. I will call back later," he said. California might as well have been on another planet since his entire existence barely went beyond Karsten Field these days. He suspected he would never set foot out of Iowa for the rest of his life.

Tina sounded different. She seemed bothered by the early morning call, but she did not have that old stress in her voice. She said, "No. No, it's okay. Why are you calling?"

"It's about my daughter," started Allan.

"Alice? Is she okay?" Tina interjected.

Allan corrected her, "No. I mean, yes. Alice is fine. I am calling about my youngest daughter, Ruth."

"Oh," came Tina's flat response. She suddenly seemed less concerned. Allan could not blame his ex-wife to not share as much enthusiasm for a child he had with another woman. However, she did not hang up, so he continued.

"My Ruth has been having fainting spells. We went to see a local doctor, Wilson, who said it might be the cause of an aneurysm. We have no medical insurance and know of no one that can help her."

Silence. It seemed to take a very long time for Tina to respond. When she did, Allan did not expect what she would say. He did not think Tina could, or would, help. He only called her because he believed God directed Alice to give him that news. She said, "I can't make any promises. Have your Dr. Wilson send Ruth's files to my husband. Do you have something to write his information on?"

While Allan waited for Mrs. Kinzinger to bring him a paper napkin, Tina had one more thing to say. "It's good to hear your voice, Allan. It's funny that you called. Last night, Hiro and I had the strangest conversation. He said he felt like something was missing from his practice. He said it has been nagging him for a while, but yesterday, it started to become clear."

Allan did not want to pry too much into Tina's personal life. He felt God at work, but now had other tasks to complete. He finished his phone call abruptly, thanked Mrs. Kinzinger and headed to tell Mary of the next step in their plan.

Dr. Wilson helped with pleasure and did not even charge any filing or copy fees. She sent the results of her examination to Tina's husband, Dr. Hiro Takamura, at his Beverly Hills office. After that, Allan expected a long wait with little information.

To his surprise and God's glory, Allan found himself back at Kinzinger's restaurant in less than a week. He and Mary sat in the corner booth across the table from Tina and Hiro. Dr. Takamura shared the story of his blessings from meeting Tina when he was starting out as a surgeon in Des Moines and growing to an in-demand specialist in Los Angeles. Financially, his practice could support them for the rest of their life even if he retired tomorrow.

"That is a problem for me," said Hiro. "I have been blessed with a talent for healing people and I have always done it within the system. I am not finding fulfillment with money alone. Tina and I agree that something is missing."

He adjusted his wire frame glasses. A strand of black hair fell into his eyes and he brushed it back into the locks trimmed with the start of silver. Allan looked from the doctor to Tina. The lines grew at the corners of her mouth and eyes. He saw a face he remembered, but did not recognize. The years had been kind to her, but it was not the same face from his memory. The look in her eyes showed a peace that was not there in their final years of marriage. She seemed happy and the constant hand-holding and shoulder-rubbing told Allan that she had a great relationship with a successful man.

Mary spoke for Allan's reluctance. "Physical gain is not why we are on this earth. Our reward awaits us in the next life."

"It has taken me a long time to understand that. I want to change that. My parents came to this country as newlyweds in the sixties. They adopted the language and the religion. I was raised as a Christian, but also the son of a businessman. Tina and I decided not to have children. We honor your decision to do so at your age," said Hiro.

Allan did not know how to take that comment. He did not feel old and did not think he was too old for more children, if it was part of God's plan. He remembered old Elder Tibold fathered a child when he was in his late sixties or so. Allan guessed he was missing the point and waited for an explanation.

Dr. Takamura continued, "My point is that Tina and I are looking for something to give us more spiritual satisfaction. It is not enough for us to be fiscally happy. We want to make God happy with our works. I have looked into several foundations that do charitable works, but there is a lot of red tape. Then last week, I had an epiphany. I would start my own foundation, set my own rules. I only needed a first patient. The next morning you called."

"Praise God," Allan said with astonishment. He thought again about Abraham and Isaac. He thought about how when he gave everything up to his Lord, those things seemed to change.

Tina explained, "We want to help Ruth. Hiro can do it with no insurance and no expense for you."

"But how would we get her to California?" asked Mary. Allan could tell his wife was not convinced.

"That is the best part," said Hiro. "You don't. I have already been in contact with a hospital in Des Moines. I still have a few friends there. I have agreed to make certain donations and they are giving me access to their facilities. To cut through the bureaucracy, it will be like you have private insurance. If they are lacking any equipment, I will donate that too."

Allan wanted to reach across the table and hug the man. He felt unable to control the smile spreading across his face. "It seems that God wants you to use your gift."

Dr. Takamura added, "Yes, but not only for the wealthy or well-insured. Tina and I have prayed a lot this past week. I am making a vow to you today that I will never decline a patient again, simply for being uninsured. Have you ever heard of a neurosurgeon that works for free? I feel strongly that God will provide for the needs of our endeavor."

Allan's infectious smile spread to the rest of the table. He could feel the Holy Spirit in their presence and they all shared a laugh and several slices of Mrs. Kinzinger's lip-puckering gooseberry pie.

Allan processed the information that came from their many visits with Dr. Takamura over the next several weeks. That did not mean he understood it all. Watching his young daughter subjected to so many tests and strange machines brought worry and fear to Allan's heart. He found strength in Ruth's confident face and hours of prayer.

Of all of them, young Ruth was the only one that never showed fear or concern. She went through each procedure with confidence. She even found delight when Dr. Wilson came to work with Dr. Takamura.

To the best of Allan's understanding, Dr. Takamura concluded that Ruth did have an aneurysm. The good news was that it would be operable and since they caught it at an early age, she should have no side-affects after its removal. He said the peculiar thing was that the swollen blood vessel pressed against a part of her brain that should have incapacitated her.

"It's a miracle that she can walk or talk," said the dedicated doctor.

Allan did not doubt it was a miracle. He always felt that God had His hand on that little girl. Since her birth, she always seemed special, but too many things happened in recent memory that told Allan there was a plan for her.

Allan also marveled at his wife. Mary stayed calm and constant during these harrowing days. Her worst moment came when the doctors said they would have to completely shave Ruth's head for the surgery. They let Mary keep as many lock of her daughter's feathery soft hair as she wanted. To their dying day, both Mary and Allan would carry a brown braid with them at all times.

On the day of the surgery, Ruth's entire family came to the hospital, even Brett and Kat. The young couple helped watch Benjamin and the twins while Alice and Samuel prayed with Allan and Mary. Dr. Takamura asked if he and Tina could pray with them before the surgery.

"I have never brought prayer into the hospital. I know people often do it, but it never seemed professional to me. I always kept my faith private. Today seems like a good day to change old habits," said Hiro.

It delighted Allan to have young Dr. Wilson join them. He would always be thankful to her for the first steps in this journey. He praised God that she risked a promising career to assist Dr. Takamura. In return, Dr. Takamura asked her to head the new practice while he wrapped up business in Los Angeles and worked on securing a future for their blessed endeavor.

So many wonderful things came together at this moment. Allan trusted in the Lord's plan, but always found amazement in how it came to fruition. All of the little details aligned exactly right for them all to be at this moment together. He knew that only the greatest force in all of existence could envision a miracle like that.

The surgery lasted longer than Allan could stand. He paced the waiting room enough to prompt Mary into saying, "Husband, you will need to re-sole those boots if you do not find peace soon."

Finally, Dr. Takamura came from the operating room with Dr. Wilson a few steps behind him. Both had taken the time to remove their plastic gloves, but neither had removed their face masks yet. Allan could not read the look in Hiro's dark eyes, obscured by the overhead fluorescents reflecting on his glasses. The tension became unbearable.

"What of my child?" Allan asked.

Dr. Takamura pulled down his thin fabric face mask to reveal a joyous smile. He said nothing, but hugged Allan. Dr. Wilson removed her mask and announced, "It was a complete success."

Between countless tears and even more *Thank You's* to God, Allan could not get used to the look of Ruth's bald head. The doctors kept bandages over the incision, but Allan had to look at least once. The sight of the stitches gave him an uneasy stomach. One look turned out to be all he needed.

As long as the hospital allowed, Allan and Mary stayed at their daughter's bedside. The young girl slept most of the day after her surgery. During that time, Allan shared with his wife many of his thoughts and prayers that brought them to this moment. He admitted while he had come to peace with the idea of their Lord calling Ruth home, he was incredibly thankful that she would be with them much longer.

Ruth awoke the first time right after Mary excused herself to the restroom. The little girl's eyes fluttered open. Without talking, her hands went straight to her head. She gingerly felt along the sides of the bandage and ran her fingers over the smooth stubble. Ruth laughed.

"Dr. Wilson said it would feel funny."

Allan tried his hardest to keep composure. He said, "It does not look funny. You are one of God's most beautiful creations with or without hair."

"Datt?"

"Yes, mein herz," said Allan.

"I don't think I can see Isaac anymore," she said.

At once, Allan felt bad for her. It had to hurt to lose a connection like that. He did not think her guardian angel would truly abandon her. However, he remembered Dr. Wilson saying it was only a hallucination. If the hallucination was gone, he believed that meant his daughter was completely cured of the ailment. Allan felt trapped somewhere between Heaven and earth. Seeing what he thought was the spirit of Isaac early that one morning made him believe.

"Don't worry. Because we cannot see him does not mean he is not there," said Allan.

"Like God?" asked Ruth.

"Yes, like God. He is always there," finished Allan.

Mary came back into the room and talk turned to hugs. Allan went for Alice, Brett and Benjamin and the whole family embraced and offered a prayer of thanks.

Because of the unusual circumstances, Dr. Takamura required Ruth to stay in the hospital longer than a typical patient. He wanted to keep her under constant watch and knew finding transportation to the hospital from Karsten Field might be difficult.

In that time, Ruth had a stream of visitors. One of her favorites came from old Mr. Zook and Miss Margaret. Ruth always liked Ben Abrim and thought they had a special connection. Ruth looked from his ever-smiling face to a bundle of papers he held in his hand.

"Praise God that I can look into your smiling eyes once again," said Ben Abrim. He set the stack of papers on Ruth's beside stand and laid a pencil across the top of the stack. Ruth thumbed through the top few pages and saw all of them were blank.

"Was is das?" said Ruth, doing her best impersonation of Ben Abrim.

"It is for you," explained Ben Abrim. "I understand you will be staying here for a while longer. Since I cannot come visit you every day, I think you should write to me a letter if you feel lonely."

Ruth crinkled up her face. "But I don't know how to write," she said.

"You have been blessed with intelligence beyond your years. Besides, I think your Mamm or that nice doctor lady will help you. Write to me whenever you have need, tomorrow or twenty years from now. You put that pencil to paper whenever life presents you with a question you cannot answer on your own. One day, I will not be here to write back to you, but I think God will carry your letter and you will find the reply you need," said Ben Abrim.

Ruth kept that pencil and paper. She wrote to Ben Abrim. She wrote when she felt lonely. She wrote when she felt confused, or scared, or happy. She shared good news and bad. Many years later, boxes of those letters, many undelivered, would be read by Ruth's grandchildren.

That, however, is another story.